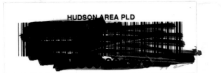
W9-BVX-424

big NATE
ALL WORK AND NO PLAY

More

big NATE

adventures from

LINCOLN PEIRCE

Novels:

Big Nate: In a Class By Himself

Big Nate Strikes Again

Big Nate On a Roll

Big Nate Goes For Broke

Activity Books:

Big Nate Boredom Buster

Big Nate Fun Blaster

Comic Compilations:

Big Nate From the Top

Big Nate Out Loud

Big Nate and Friends

Big Nate: What Could Possibly Go Wrong?

Big Nate: Here Goes Nothing

Big Nate Makes the Grade

big NATE
ALL WORK AND NO PLAY

A COLLECTION OF SUNDAYS

by LINCOLN PEIRCE

Andrews McMeel
Publishing, LLC

Kansas City • Sydney • London

Big Nate is distributed internationally by Universal Uclick.

Big Nate All Work and No Play copyright © 2012 by United Feature Syndicate, Inc. All rights reserved. Printed in the United States of America. No part of this book may be used or reproduced in any manner whatsoever without written permission except in the case of reprints in the context of reviews.

Andrews McMeel Publishing, LLC
an Andrews McMeel Universal company
1130 Walnut Street, Kansas City, Missouri 64106

www.andrewsmcmeel.com

12 13 14 15 16 BAM 10 9 8 7 6 5 4 3 2

ISBN: 978-1-4494-2567-8

Library of Congress Control Number: 2012936727

ATTENTION: SCHOOLS AND BUSINESSES
Andrews McMeel books are available at quantity discounts with bulk purchase for educational, business, or sales promotional use. For information, please e-mail the Andrews McMeel Publishing Special Sales Department: specialsales@amuniversal.com

BIG NATE

by Lincoln Peirce

MAN! IT'S POURING OUT THERE!

DANG! WE CAN'T SHOOT HOOPS IN THIS!

BUT HERE'S SOMETHING WE CAN DO!

WE CAN LOOK AT MY WORLD-FAMOUS "CHEEZ DOODLE" COLLECTION!

LET'S START WITH THIS ONE! IT'S PERFECTLY STRAIGHT INSTEAD OF CURVED! PRETTY UNUSUAL, EH?

...OR HOW ABOUT THIS! FIVE DOODLES, MAGICALLY LINKED TOGETHER IN A CHEESY, CRUNCHY CHAIN!

HERE'S SOMETHING YOU DON'T SEE EVERY DAY! A DOODLE WITH A HOLE IN IT! I ALMOST FAINTED WHEN I SAW THIS!

✳CHUCKLE!✳ THIS ONE'S FUNNY! IT'S SHAPED LIKE THE HEAD OF ABE LINCOLN! UNCANNY, HUH?

NOW, IF CHEEZ DOODLES COULD TALK, THIS NEXT ONE WOULD HAVE QUITE A STORY TO—

?

by Lincoln Peirce

OH!...DADDY! WILL YOU LET ME KNOW WHEN GORDIE GETS HERE?

HE'S ALREADY HERE, HON.

HE IS?

I'VE BEEN CALLING YOU! GORDIE'S DOWNSTAIRS!

BY HIMSELF? DAAAAAAD! GO KEEP HIM COMPANY!

OH, HE'S NOT BY HIMSELF! NATE'S DOWN THERE WITH HIM!

I THINK THEY'RE LOOKING AT PHOTOS!

!

NAAAAAATE!

UH... I THINK YOUR SISTER WANTS YOU.

YEAH, YEAH. NOW THIS IS ELLEN DURING HER UNFORTUNATE "PUDGY" PHASE...

8

BIG NATE by Lincoln Peirce

...TWO...

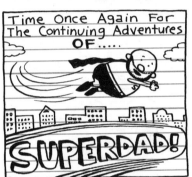

Time Once Again For The Continuing Adventures OF..... **SUPERDAD!**

Simply put, **SUPERDAD** isn't like other, better-known superheroes!

He's not **FAST!**

Hello? HELLO?

Dang! They hung up!

He's not **STRONG!**

MAN, this remote is heavy!

He's.... well... **LOOK at him!**

"Apply Rogaine To Affected Area"...

But he **IS** a superhero! Which means when someone is in need... **HE RESPONDS!**

Time to change into my **SUPERDAD** costume!

Yes, he **RESPONDS!**

I said... he **RESPONDS!**

Uh... hello?

ANY DAY NOW, DAD.

FITTING ROOM 3

❊OOF!❊ SOMETHING'S WRONG!... THIS **CAN'T** BE A 34-INCH WAIST!

SALE

---

big NATE

by Lincoln Peirce

Hello, friends! My special guest today is none other than famed sleep-meister... **MISTER SANDMAN!**

Call me "Sandy," Chip.

So, Sandy... You're in charge of helping people fall asleep, am I right?

Not **ALL** people, Chip! My area of expertise is **children**!

I see... and is it difficult to get children to sleep?

It CAN be! There are a lot of factors to consider!

Such as?

Well, like SUGAR! You let a kid eat ice cream before bed, and **I'M** in for a long night!

SLUMBER PARTIES are brutal, too! Ever try to get a dozen ten-year-olds to fall asleep at the same time?

Uh...no.

The **SEASON** has a lot to do with it, too! At **THIS** time of year, it's almost **IMPOSSIBLE** for kids to get a good night's sleep!

Why's that?

WELLLLLCOME BAAAAACK!

NO! NO! NO!

10

big NATE
by Lincoln Peirce

Sir? You'll have to buy those pants.

SALE

WHATCHA DOIN', SON?

DRAWING COMICS.

WHAT KIND OF COMICS?

I DUNNO. JUST COMICS.

FUNNY COMICS? OR ACTION COMICS?

OH.... BOTH, SORT OF.

WELL, THEN... IS IT A LONG, AMBITIOUS STORY LIKE A COMIC BOOK, OR—?

I WAS JUST LOOKING FOR A WAY TO PASS THE TIME, THAT'S ALL.

ARE YOU MAKING UP SOME NEW CHARACTERS?

NO, NO... IT'S NOTHING SPECIAL.

IT'S JUST A COMIC! A REGULAR COMIC, JUST LIKE I DRAW EVERY DAY!

"DAD'S REAL LIFE COMICS! EPISODE 6: A HUMILIATING INCIDENT IN A DRESSING ROOM AT THE GAP."

SEE? SAME OLD SAME OLD.

BY Lincoln Peirce

The LAST Summer Blockbuster... EVER!!

DAY OF RECKONING!

starring: MOE MENTUM!

Washington, August 1998:

WHAT?? A giant asteroid is on a collision course with Earth?

Right, Mr. President! Only **ONE MAN** can save us!...

SLADE McSUEDE, soldier of fortune!

Give me a plane, a jackknife, and a box of baking soda, and I'll stop that asteroid **COLD**!

AND SOON...

Houston, this is McSuede. I'm about to blow this asteroid to kingdom come!

Roger, McSuede!

USA

?!?! oh, NO! My missiles aren't firing!

Backup systems have failed!

DO something, McSuede!

TOO LATE! The asteroid is entering Earth's atmosphere!

THE EARTH IS DOO...

AAAAAH! I SMUDGED!

OH, IT'S NOT THE END OF THE WORLD.

by Lincoln Peirce

RRRRINNNNGGG

BACK-to-SCHOOL **HIP-HOP!**

with master rapper: **"FLUFF DADDY"!**

Let me tell you folks a story,
Won't you lend me an **EAR**!
'Cause the day I've waited for
The whole dang summer is **HERE**!
As the leaves begin to tumble
And the weather turns **COOL**,
Need I say it? (Sure I'll say it!)
Nate goes **BACK TO SCHOOL**!

It's a day I get to party but it makes Nate **PANIC**!
It reminds me, just a little, of that flick "**TITANIC**"!
During summer, Nate was sailing on a luxury **SHIP**
But today he'll hit an iceberg with a kung-fu **GRIP**!

CRACK!

Mrs. Godfrey is the reason
For his feelings of dread,
'Cause the woman feasts on students
(And she's very well-fed).
How do **I** feel that my son
Has such a teacher as she?
Let me put it to you this way:
Better **HIM** than **ME**!

While he's dealing with a woman
Who's a sociopath,
I'll be watching "Jerry Springer"
As I lounge in the bath!
While he's doing all the work,
"Fluff Dad" will do all the play!
While he's toiling in the classroom, **I** will...

HAVE A GREAT DAY!

big NATE

by Lincoln Peirce

FIELD GOAL!

BOOT!

HUDDLE UP!

HUDDLE UP!

YOU WANNA START OFF AS RECEIVER OR QB?

I'LL BE QB!

OKAY, I'LL GO OUT! I'LL RUN FIVE STEPS UP THE LEFT SIDELINE...

...THEN I'LL ZIG TO THE INSIDE, ZAG TO THE OUTSIDE, THEN...

TEDDY! TEDDY!

YOU'RE GETTING TOO **COMPLICATED!** LOOK WHO'S PLAYING DEFENSE! YOU DON'T EVEN **NEED** A PATTERN!

THIS GUY'S **PATHETIC!** IF YOU JUST RUN IN A STRAIGHT LINE, YOU'LL BLOW RIGHT BY HIM!

I CAN HEAR YOU!!

EITHER THAT, OR HE'LL FALL DOWN!

by Lincoln Peirce

THERE'S NIGHTMARES, AND THEN THERE'S NIGHTMARES.

SHLOX-TV presents... **"I WANT TO BE A JILLIONAIRE!"** APPLAU with your host: **KEN DOOLITTLE!**

Friends, let's welcome our next contestant: 15-year-old cheerleader and "Dilly Burger" employee **ELLEN WRIGHT!!** CLAP! CLAP! CLAP! CLAP! CLAP!

Ellen... **GOOD LUCK!** Now HERE'S your FIRST QUESTION!

"Little Miss Muffet sat on a..." **BLANK!** Is the answer A. swing B. hilltop C. chair, or D. tuffet

TICK TICK TICK TICK TICK TICK TICK TICK TICK TICK TICK TICK ? ? ? ?

Uh... Ellen? Yes, Don? It's Ken. Yes, Ken?

Do you guess A, B, C or D? I'll guess B, Don. Is that your... FINAL ANSWER? What does "final answer" mean?

BZZZZZZ! AWWWWW! **SORRY,** Ellen! You should have used your "lifeline"! What's that?

That's when you admit you're not **SMART** enough to answer the question your**SELF**... ...so you REACH OUT to someone you KNOW!

I'M REACHING OUT TO SOMEONE I KNOW.

big NATE

by Lincoln Peirce

Panel 1:

Time For Another Edition Of...
CELEBRITY INTERVIEW!
with your host:
Chip Chipson

Today's Guest:
Celebrity Psychic
CLAIRE VOYANT!

Panel 2:

Greetings, Friends! Today psychic **CLAIRE VOYANT** will make some **PREDICTIONS** about the coming school year!

I knew you were going to say that.

Panel 3:

Claire, what's in the future for everyone's favorite 6th-grade Renaissance Man, **NATE WRIGHT**?

Hmm...

Panel 4:

Nate will be lucky in love. He will be awash in a virtual "babe tsunami."

animal magnetism

Panel 5:

His prodigious athletic skills will bring him great success on the playing field.

Look! NATE'S playing goal!

Why even try?

We forfeit.

Panel 6:

But...hmm...in Nate's **IMMEDIATE** future, something else is coming into focus!... a NUMBER!

Panel 7:

What kind of number, Claire?

Still hazy... It... it's a two-digit number! A **LOW** two-digit number!

Panel 8:

A **12**?

FOR THE NEXT TEST, AT LEAST **PRETEND** TO STUDY.

big NATE

by Lincoln Peirce

HI, KATHY!

HI, NATE!

COVERING THE GAME FOR THE SCHOOL PAPER?

YUP!

MAKE SURE YOU PUT SOME GOOD STUFF ABOUT **ME** IN YOUR ARTICLE!

AFTER ALL...AS GOALIE, I'M THE **BACKBONE** OF THE TEAM!

I'M THE LAST LINE OF DEFENSE!... THE ANCHOR!... THE **ROCK**!

HEY, MAYBE YOU COULD EVEN PUT ME IN THE **HEADLINE**!!

I CAN ALMOST GUARANTEE IT.

OOH! HEAR THAT, GUYS? I'M A CELEBRITY!

BIG NATE

by Lincoln Peirce

YOU KNOW WHAT'S FUN? STIRRING UP CONTROVERSY AMONG THE FACULTY!

DETENTION

✷ AHEM! ✷ HI, MRS. CZERWICKI!

SIT DOWN, NATE.

YOU KNOW, MRS. CZERWICKI, I WAS JUST THINKING ABOUT YOUR ROLE AS DETENTION MONITOR... IT JUST DOESN'T SEEM FAIR!

IT'S THE **CLASSROOM** TEACHERS WHO HAND OUT THE DETENTIONS! BUT **YOU'RE** THE ONE LEFT SITTING HERE AFTER SCHOOL!

THE TEACHERS DROP **THEIR** PROBLEMS IN **YOUR** LAP! I, FOR ONE, AM **OUTRAGED** AT THE WAY THEY TAKE ADVANTAGE OF YOU!

YOU KNOW, NATE, YOU HAVE A POINT.

PERHAPS INSTEAD OF SITTING HERE WITH ME, YOU SHOULD BE SPENDING TIME WITH THE TEACHER WHO SENT YOU HERE.

SOUNDS LIKE SOME SORT OF PARTY IN THE DETENTION ROOM.

DETENTION

20

big NATE

by Lincoln Peirce

HEY! CAN I PLAY?

OH, NO...

Time Once Again For...
"FEELINGS"
with your host:
DR. WARREN FUZZY!

Greetings, soul travelers!

Friends, I'm here today to talk about a common but serious condition among middle-aged men: "PETER PAN SYNDROME"!

Peter Pan, of course, is the beloved hero of children's literature who simply REFUSES to grow up!

Likewise, the world is **FULL** of men who are determined **NOT** to act their age!

examples:

comb-over

trophy wife

Desperate to recapture their youth, they feebly attempt to act 'like the boys they once were, unaware of just how **PATHETIC** they look!

Word up, homeys!

How can we help these poor souls? The answer is surprisingly simple: by doing **NOTHING**!!

These men **CAN'T** turn back Time! Eventually, reality will set in and they'll discover the cruel truth: they're **OLD!**

⌗GASP!⌗... WHEEZE... G-GOING... INSIDE...

FINALLY.

21

BIG NATE

by Lincoln Peirce

HEAR ME, DEMONS OF DARKNESS!

RRRRIINNNNGGG

THERE'S THE BELL! DAY OVER!

TIME FOR OUR FIRST CARTOONING CLUB MEETING OF THE YEAR!

YESSS! THE ONE PART OF SCHOOL I LOOKED FORWARD TO ALL SUMMER!

I MUST SAY, WE HAVE THE BEST CLUB IN SCHOOL! BY **FAR**!

HEY, WAIT'LL YOU SEE THE COMIC STRIP I'M GONNA DRAW ABOUT MRS. GODFREY!

HEE HEE! I'VE GOT A FEW PLANS FOR HER MYSELF!

BOYS! HANG ON A SEC!

HI, MR. ROSA! ON YOUR WAY TO THE CARTOONING CLUB?

NOT TODAY, I'M AFRAID! I'VE GOT A DENTIST APPOINTMENT I'VE ALREADY RESCHEDULED THREE TIMES!

BUT THE CLUB CAN STILL MEET! I ASKED ANOTHER TEACHER TO FILL IN FOR ME AS YOUR ADVISOR! OKAY?

OKAY! THANKS!

CARTOONING CLUB! TODAY 3:00

HELLO, BOYS.

OH, HOW I HATE HER.

WISDOM

WELCOME TO PEER COUNSELING, GUYS! WHAT'S THE PROBLEM?

"LET'S WORK IT OUT"

WELL, I DID THIS DRAWING DURING STUDY HALL...

IT WASN'T JUST **YOU**! WE **BOTH** WORKED ON IT!

IT'S **MY** DRAWING! ALL YOU DID WAS THE HANDS AND HELMET!

THAT'S A **LOT**! IT'S **MY** DRAWING, **TOO**!

GUYS, **GUYS**! LET'S GET THIS RESOLVED! GIVE ME THE DRAWING AND SIT DOWN!

THIS IS WHAT ALL THE FUSS IS ABOUT? ✳SMIRK!✳ NO OFFENSE, GUYS, BUT THIS ISN'T EXACTLY A PICASSO!

WELL, ANYWAY... THERE'S ONLY ONE WAY TO DETERMINE WHO OWNS THIS DRAWING!

WE DIVIDE IT IN **HALF**!

RRR- RIP!

WHAT'S THE MESSAGE HERE, YOU ASK? **COOPERATE** WITH EACH OTHER! **SHARE** EXPERIENCES! **WORK TOGETHER**!

WANNA HAVE A TURN?

HEY, THANKS!

by Lincoln Peirce

LASSIE

SPITSY

ALL RIGHT, SPITSY, LET'S GO FOR A WALK!

HOLD **STILL**, WILL YOU? LET ME GET THIS LEASH ON!

WHOA! SPITSY! STOP! DOWN, BOY! HEEL!!

DANG, SPITSY! YOU ALMOST RIPPED MY **ARM** OFF! COOL YOUR JETS, WILL Y—

YANK!

OKAY, OKAY! I'LL LET YOU RUN FREE! BUT DON'T DO ANY—

ZOOM!

BANG! CRASH!

SPITSY!... **NO!** THAT'S SOMEBODY'S **GARBAGE!**

CHOMPF! SLUP!

LET'S GET OUT OF HERE BEFORE ANY—

!

BAD, BAD, BAD, BAD, BAD, BAD, BAD, BAD, BAD, BAD, BAD, BAD, BAD, BAD, BAD DOG.

GODFREY

big NATE
by Lincoln Peirce

HIKE!

WRIGHT

MUNCH
MUNCH
MUNCH

SLAM!

PERHAPS YOU MISUNDERSTOOD ME WHEN I SAID "GO LONG."

I DIDN'T WANT TO PLAY ANYMORE.

25

BIG NATE

by Lincoln Peirce

MR. ROSA! CAN WE EAT LUNCH IN HERE?

SURE, GUYS!

IT'S NICE TO BE THE SORT OF TEACHER KIDS FEEL **COMFORTABLE** WITH!

THERE AREN'T MANY CLASSROOMS THEY ACTUALLY **WANT** TO HANG OUT IN!

YAK YAK!

OF COURSE, NOT MANY TEACHERS ARE AS WELL-LIKED BY THE STUDENTS AS I AM!

THEN AGAIN, YOU'VE GOT TO BE CAREFUL THEY DON'T LIKE YOU **TOO** MUCH!

CHATTER CHATTER BLAH BLAH

YOU CAN'T LET STUDENTS FORGET WHO'S BOSS!

I'LL JUST GIVE THEM A FIRM REMINDER...

YAK YAK YAK

❊AHEM!❊ BOYS, QUIET DOWN OR I'LL HAVE TO ASK YOU TO LEAVE.

WA HA HA HA HA HA HA HA HA HA H

...BEFORE IT'S TOO LATE.

HEE HEE! OH, MAN!

GOOD ONE, KEN! CAN I CALL YOU KEN?

big NATE

by Lincoln Peirce

Hello, friends! CHIP CHIPSON here with a special report: **AT HOME WITH MRS. GODFREY!!**

Mrs. G., a lot of people are wondering: what's your life like AWAY from the classroom? Will you show us around?

Sure, Chip.

E-GAD! A jar of slugs and maggots!

Careful, you fool! That's my dinner!

Nice... um... coffin.

I need a firm mattress.

here?

WAP!

$$\frac{17}{102} = \frac{x}{36}$$

$12 \times \frac{5}{6} \ \ \ \frac{120}{}$

$$\begin{array}{r} \cdot 36 \\ 17 \\ \hline 252 \\ 360 \\ \hline 612 \end{array} \quad \begin{array}{r} 60 \\ 10 \end{array}$$

$102\overline{)612}$

WELL, NATE, I'M GLAD TO SEE YOU WORKING SO HARD.

UNFORTUNATELY YOU'RE WORKING ON **MATH**. THIS IS **SOCIAL STUDIES**.

I WHIPPED OUT THE WRONG DECOY SHEET.

ARE THOSE **DRAWINGS** UNDER THERE?

A BANANA PEEL?

YUP! I'VE GOT A POINT TO PROVE!

HAVE YOU EVER SEEN — **REALLY** SEEN — SOMEONE SLIP ON A BANANA PEEL?

WELL, IN CARTOONS I'VE—

AH-**HA!** IN **CARTOONS!** BUT NOT IN REAL LIFE!

...AND WHY NOT? BECAUSE BANANA PEELS ARE **NOT** SLIPPERY!

SEE? I COULDN'T SLIP ON THIS IF I **TRIED!**

HMM! YOU'RE RIGHT!

ANOTHER EXAMPLE OF PEOPLE BELIEVING A **MYTH!**

PEOPLE JUST DON'T SLIP ON BANANA PEELS IN REAL LIFE! IT **DOESN'T HAPPEN!**

ZZUP!

THIS ISN'T HAPPENING.

SHUT UP

PRINCIPAL

bIG NATE

by Lincoln Peirce

HELLO, friends! **BIFF BIFFWELL** here! Time for our annual conversation with **HOWARD PLOTZ**, resolution accountant!

Yo, Biff.

As we all know, **HOWARD** here keeps track of all the New Year's Resolutions that people make at this time of year!

Correct

Tell me, Howard. Do people get in trouble when they break a resolution?

Not always, Biff

Some resolutions simply **CAN'T** be kept! They're **MADE** to be broken!

And why's that?

Because they're made under **DURESS**! Usually at the suggestion of a misguided **PARENT**!

What ends up happening? People make resolutions they really **DON'T WANT** to keep!

So... it's **OKAY** to break those kinds of resolutions?

ABSOLUTELY, Biff! To do otherwise would be **UNNATURAL**!

I GOTTA BE ME!

PITY.

Hello, Folks! My name's **KEN DOLITTLE!** Welcome to... **THIS IS YOUR LIFE!**

CLAP! CLAP! CLAP! CLAP!

...And our special guest today is... **DAD!** Guess what, Dad? **THIS IS YOUR LIFE!**

What's a life?

Dad, we've searched the country for friends and neighbors from your past!...People who want to tell you just how much you've **MEANT** to them over the years!

And now it's time to **MEET** those friends and neighbors! Let's bring 'em in, Johnny!

Uh... Johnny?

Yeah, Ken?

ON THE AIR

Where are the friends from Dad's past?

We couldn't find any, Ken.

WHAT ARE YOU WORKING ON?

!

THIS IS MY LIFE.

big NATE by Lincoln Peirce

WHAT WAS THE "MAGNA CARTA"? WHO CAN TELL US?

NATE?

ME? BUT I DIDN'T EVEN HAVE MY HAND UP!

YES, I KNOW.

BY SLUMPING DOWN BEHIND YOUR DESK TO AVOID BEING CALLED ON, YOU ACTUALLY DREW **MORE** ATTENTION TO YOURSELF.

THINK ABOUT IT.

WHO CAN TELL US SOMETHING ABOUT THE "STAMP ACT"?

NATE?

ME?

DID YOU OR DID YOU NOT HAVE YOUR HAND UP?

PSST! YOU'RE SLUMPING AGAIN.

NO, I'M JUST BEATEN DOWN...

big NATE

by Lincoln Peirce

OW.

CARTOON-
ING
CLUB
Meeting
TODAY!
ROOM
215

GANG, AS YOUR FACULTY ADVISOR, I WANT TO AD-DRESS SOME CON-CERNS ABOUT YOUR CARTOONS.

I'VE NOTICED THAT MANY OF YOU SPEND A LOT OF TIME DRAW-ING CARTOONS ABOUT YOUR CLASSMATES.

THE PROBLEM IS THAT THESE CARTOONS ARE OFTEN CRUEL!... EVEN **VICIOUS**!

THERE'S NOTHING FUNNY ABOUT BELITTLING OTHERS FOR YOUR OWN ENJOYMENT! DO YOU HAVE TO MAKE OTHERS FEEL BAD SO THAT **YOU** CAN FEEL GOOD?

STARTING TODAY, I'M IMPOSING A NEW RULE: NO MORE COMICS ABOUT YOUR CLASSMATES!

OKAY? HAVE FUN.

Don't be mean!

Be perfect like me!

DUHH..

I DON'T MEAN TO BE "PICKY," BUT...

MR...

Dang!

OW!

jug ears

NATE! WHAT ARE YOU DOING HERE?

SELLING COOKIES FOR MY SCOUT TROOP, MRS. GODFREY!

SELLING COOKIES? WITH THE AMOUNT OF HOMEWORK I GAVE YOU THIS WEEKEND?

OH, RIGHT... THE HOMEWORK...

I ASSUME YOU'VE FINISHED IT.

UH... WELL... NOT EXACTLY.

NOT EXACTLY? HAVE YOU EVEN STARTED IT?

UH... **SURE** I HAVE! I'M... I'M ALMOST DONE!

BUT YOU'RE **NOT** DONE! AND YET YOU'RE GALAVANTING AROUND THE NEIGHBORHOOD IN YOUR SCOUT UNIFORM!

I GUESS YOU CARE MORE ABOUT SELLING **COOKIES** THAN YOU DO YOUR SOCIAL STUDIES GRADE!

WELL, I... **NO!** NO, NOT AT ALL!

OH, REALLY? SO YOU'RE SAYING YOU'LL CHANGE YOUR WAYS? YOU'LL PUT YOUR HOMEWORK **FIRST** FROM NOW ON?

NOW YOU KNOW WHY SCOUTING TEACHES US SURVIVAL SKILLS!

OH, HOW I HATE HER.

NATE!... NATE! WAKE UP!

HMM?

YOU WERE TALKING IN YOUR SLEEP!

SMAK! SMAK!

WHO DO YOU THINK YOU ARE, YOUNG MAN?

ME?

I GUESS I'M JUST ANOTHER STUDENT WHO'S BORED SILLY BY THIS LAME CLASS.

⚡GASP!⚡

NOBODY ELSE HAS THE GUTS TO SAY THIS, SO **I WILL**: MRS. GODFREY, YOUR LECTURES ARE ABOUT AS INTERESTING AS A BAG OF WET SAND.

YOU'VE GOT TO BE THE WORST TEACHER OF ALL TIME! HAVE YOU EVER CONSIDERED A CAREER IN SUMO?

...AND FOR YOUR INFORMATION, I DO **NOT** TALK IN MY SLEEP!

ARE YOU SURE ABOUT THAT?

HMM? ABSOLUTELY.

big NATE

by Lincoln Peirce

KSSSCH!

SO YOU STILL CLAIM YOU CAN FIND ANYTHING IN THIS MESS?

ANYTHING!

NATE! DO YOU HAVE THAT CHESS ARTICLE I ASKED YOU ABOUT?

SURE DO!

RUSTLE RUSTLE RUSTLE

HERE YA GO!

THANKS

NATE, I NEED A COPY OF THE GETTYSBURG ADDRESS FOR MY REPORT!

NO PROBLEM!

RUSTLE RUSTLE RUSTLE

VOILA!

THANKS!

NATE! I'M LOOKING FOR THE RULES AND REGULATIONS GOVERNING THE SPORT OF CURLING!

UN MOMENTO!

THANKS!

KRINNGG

TIME FOR MATH.

GOT YOUR HOMEWORK?

IT'S THE ONE TINY FLAW IN HIS SYSTEM.

WHERE IS IT?

by Lincoln Peirce

1.) Carl is taking a math test. There are 10 questions which take 30 seconds each; 15 questions which take 40 seconds each; and 12 questions which take two minutes each.

Carl pauses for 5 seconds between questions. In addition, he sharpens his pencil twice, which takes 20 seconds each time. The test begins promptly at 10:00 am. When Carl hands in his completed test,

what time is it?

YAAAAAAAH!

HEAVE!

RRRRRRRR

ROWF ROWF
ROWF ROWF
ROWF
ROWF

YANK!

YIP!

PHEEEEW!...

WAM!

FOOTBALL INJURY.

WOW... YOU POOR BABY!

big NATE

by Lincoln Peirce

Z...

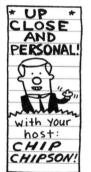

UP CLOSE AND PERSONAL!

"..." with your host: *CHIP CHIPSON!*

Greetings, friends! I'm here with "Cucurbita Pepo," or as he's more commonly known...

PAT PUMPKIN!

You da man, Chip.

Well, Pat, it's almost Halloween!

FINALLY! I'm sick of sitting around like a... a VEGETABLE!

So you look forward to this time of year, eh?

Oh, my Gourd, YES! It's the highlight of our year!

There's no greater honor for a pumpkin than getting picked, taken home and carved into a first-class Jack-o'-Lantern!

So it's not SCARY getting carved up?

Not at all! Unless... Unless...

Unless WHAT?

Unless you end up with a CLUMSY CARVER! You see, most people can easily carve a reasonably attractive pumpkin face...

...But there ARE a few hacks out there who don't know what they're doing! Getting carved by one of THEM is every pumpkin's greatest fear!

I HAD A LITTLE TROUBLE WITH THE MOUTH...

YOU'RE BLEEDING.

38

big NATE by Lincoln Peirce

MMMM!... NATE'S HALLOWEEN CANDY!

JUST A LITTLE TREAT TO KEEP ME GOING...

WAIT A MINUTE! WHAT AM I **THINKING?**

bonk bonk

THE LAST THING THIS GUT NEEDS IS ANOTHER PIECE OF JUNK FOOD!

PAT PAT

STILL... IT WOULD JUST BE **ONE** PIECE...

WHO'S IT GOING TO HURT?

TRIP!

CLANG CLANG CLANG CLANG CLANG CLANG

OW.

PAY UP.

BiG NATE

by Lincoln Peirce

Panel 1:

Time For Another Edition Of.....

CELEBRITY INTERVIEW!

with your host: *BIFF BIFFWELL!*

Panel 2:

Greetings, friends! I'm here today with everyone's favorite gourd... JACK O'LANTERN, the Halloween pumpkin!!

groannn...

Jack, Halloween has been over for **TWO WEEKS**, and I'm sure a lot of folks are wondering: How are you doing?

How am I doing? How am **I DOING?**

I'm **ROTTING**, that's how I'm doing! My once-hard exterior is turning soft and slimy! I'm covered with **MOLD!**

Panel 5:

Hmm... Yes, so I see...

Oh, **DO** you? You have no **IDEA** what we pumpkins go through!

Panel 6:

We wait **ALL YEAR** for Halloween!... And then, when it's over, what happens to us? We're **ABANDONED!**... FORGOTTEN!

Panel 7:

I can't **TAKE** it anymore! I'm gonna go out tonight and... and...

Panel 8:

Get smashed?

I'm a shell of my former self.

BIG NATE

by Lincoln Peirce

...AND ON THIS DATE IN HISTORY... UM... HMM.... LET'S SEE HERE...

☆ *Celebrity* ☆
INTERVIEW!
☆ ☆ ☆

WITH YOUR HOST: *BIFF BIFFWELL!*

Hi again, friends! **BIFF BIFFWELL** here with our special guest: **NOVEMBER 15TH!!**

Salutations, Biff.

So, 15TH, I understand you're not a happy camper.

That's correct, Biff. Nobody appreciates me!

People always take notice of **OTHER** days in November: **ELECTION DAY!**... **VETERANS** Day!... And of course that arrogant glory hound, **THANKSGIVING!**

But do people pay any attention to **ME**? **NO!** They say, "Oh, November 15th is just another day!"

But... **AREN'T** you just another day?

The point is, I could be so much **MORE**! I just need something to **HAPPEN**!

Like what?

ANYTHING! Anything **IMPORTANT!** Then people would start to recognize November 15TH as a **SPECIAL DAY!**

"NOVEMBER 15TH: SCRUB TOILETS."

GREAT.

42

BiG NATE

by Lincoln Peirce

Greetings, fulfillment-seekers! Dr. **WARREN FUZZY** here, inviting **you** and your mate to take this quiz and ask yourselves:

ARE WE "CO-DEPENDENT"?

---

① When in public together, my mate and I:

SMAK SLURP

Oh, man! Not again!

horrified bystander →

Ⓐ are proud to be seen in each other's company;
Ⓑ enjoy our mutual interests and hobbies with peers;
Ⓒ inevitably succumb to the urge to play "pass the gum."

---

② My mate and I get along so well because:

Ⓐ We respect and admire each other;
Ⓑ we share the same morals and values;
Ⓒ we wear matching outfits.

---

③ Before I met my mate, I was:

SWOON

Ⓐ happy and well-adjusted;
Ⓑ unaware I could love another person so much;
Ⓒ I have repressed that entire meaningless time of my life from my memory.

---

④ Our other friends:

Who are THEY?

Beats me.

invisible bubble

Ⓐ are happy that we are so perfect together;
Ⓑ enjoy spending time with the two of us;
Ⓒ What are "other friends"?

---

⑤ The world would be a better place if:

Ⓐ we could eradicate hunger;
Ⓑ all wars would cease;
Ⓒ The world cannot get any better because the two of us will be together forever and ever!

...AND EVER... AND EVER...

OH, GORDIE...

HEY, **VELCRO COUPLE!** WANNA TAKE A QUIZ?

BIG NATE

by Lincoln Peirce

Panel 1:
...SO THEN THE DUCK SAYS TO THE ASTRONAUT...

Panel 2:
HEY, WHAT ARE YOU DOING? CUT IT OUT!

I'M JUST GETTING THIS HAIR OFF YOUR SHOULDER...

Panel 3:
WOW! A **LONG** HAIR! A **GIRL'S** HAIR!

OOOOH! GIVE ME THAT!

Panel 4:
WHOSE HAIR IS IT, STUD?

WOULDN'T **YOU** LIKE TO KNOW!

COME ON, NATE! TELL US!

Panel 5:
OH, I THINK I'LL JUST LET YOU **GUESS!** AFTER ALL, THERE ARE PLENTY OF POSSIBILITIES! **LOTS** OF CUTE GIRLS LIKE GETTING CLOSE TO ME!

Panel 6:
✶ SNIFF! ✶...THIS FRAGRANT STRAND COULD HAVE COME FROM TINA, OR JULIE, OR SARAH...

I DON'T THINK SO...

Panel 7:
THIS HAIR HAS SOME **GRAY** IN IT!

Panel 8:
SOON I MAY BE GETTING A FEW GRAY ONES MYSELF.

44

JOHN!... BETH!

HI, NATE!

YOU TWO ARE THE LONGEST-RUNNING COUPLE IN SCHOOL! CAN I INTERVIEW YOU FOR MY GOSSIP COLUMN, "CLASSROOM CHATTER"?

SURE!

GREAT! FIRST QUESTION: WHAT MAKES YOU SUCH A GREAT COUPLE?

WE JUST GET ALONG GREAT, THAT'S ALL! I'VE NEVER LIKED ANYONE AS MUCH AS I LIKE BETH!

NOT EVEN JULIE?

UH... JULIE?

EVERYONE KNOWS HOW HOT AND HEAVY YOU AND JULIE WERE BEFORE BETH MOVED TO TOWN!

NOT EVERYONE.

OH, YEAH! THE TWO OF THEM WERE LIKE VELCRO!

B-BUT THAT WAS A YEAR AGO!

YOU NEVER TOLD ME ANYTHING ABOUT JULIE! I DON'T KEEP SECRETS FROM YOU!

OH, YEAH? WHAT ABOUT KEVIN?

I'VE TOLD YOU A MILLION TIMES! WE WERE JUST FRIENDS!

I'LL JUST PUT "NO COMMENT."

HE'S THE TYPHOID MARY OF JOURNALISM.

BIG NATE

by Lincoln Peirce

boink!

NYUK NYUK NYUK!

WHAT DO YOU THINK, GORDIE?

HMMM...

YOUR ARTWORK IS DEFINITELY IMPROVING, NATE... BUT YOUR WRITING STILL NEEDS WORK!

EVER HEARD THE SAYING THAT BASEBALL IS 90% PITCHING? DRAWING A COMIC STRIP IS 90% WRITING!

A GOOD GAG IS THE FOUNDATION! THEN YOU CAN BUILD ON THAT FOUNDATION WITH YOUR ARTWORK!

THAT MAKES SENSE.

BUT IT'S EASY TO FORGET! SOMETIMES I START DRAWING A STRIP WITHOUT KNOWING HOW IT'LL END!

I GET TO THE LAST PANEL AND I REALIZE: HEY, I DON'T HAVE A PUNCHLINE HERE!

WOW. SO WHAT DO YOU DO THEN?

WELL, SOMETIMES I RESORT TO SLAPSTICK.

BUT... ISN'T THAT SORT OF CHEAP?

SORT OF, YEAH.

big NATE
by Lincoln Peirce

HAVE YOU EVER REALLY THOUGHT ABOUT HOW UNFAIR SCHOOL IS?

THE STUDENTS HAVE NO RIGHTS! IT'S THE TEACHERS WHO TELL US WHAT TO DO, WHEN TO DO IT, WHERE TO GO!

A BELL RINGS: WE GO TO HOMEROOM! ANOTHER BELL RINGS: WE GO TO LUNCH! ANOTHER BELL RINGS! WE GO TO SOCIAL STUDIES!

ALL THESE BELLS ARE THEIR WAY TO CONTROL US! THEY'RE THE GUARDS! WE'RE THE PRISONERS!

I NEVER THOUGHT OF IT THAT WAY...

RRRRIIIINNNGG

OOP! TIME FOR MATH!

NO! DON'T GO!

RRRRRRRRRRRIIIIIIIINNNNNNGGGGGGGG

IGNORE THAT BELL! TAKE BACK CONTROL OF YOUR LIVES!!

OH, NATE! YOU'RE WONDERFUL!

RIIIIIIIIIIINNNNNNNGGGGGGGG

STAND YOUR GROUND!

NATE!... NATE!... NATE!

NATE! NATE!

DANG!

HA! THAT'S AN "E"!

JUST ONE MORE LETTER AND YOU LOSE!

I KNOW, I KNOW.

YESSS! MAKE **THAT** ONE, PAL!

RATS!

THAT'S IT! THAT'S A "Y"!

G-O-D-F-R-E-Y!

♪ FRANCIS IS A GODFREY!... FRANCIS IS A GODFREY! ♪

OH, THE **HORROR!** COULD THERE BE **ANYTHING** WORSE THAN BEING A GODFRE—

!

MY DAD SAYS THAT WHEN HE WAS A KID, THEY CALLED IT "HORSE."

by Lincoln Peirce

HOW MUCH WILL YOU GIVE ME IF I HIT THAT TREE?

THAT TREE? IT'S LIKE A HUNDRED YARDS AWAY!

WILL YOU GIVE ME TEN BUCKS?

NO, I WON'T GIVE YOU TEN BUCKS!

FIVE BUCKS?

I DON'T HAVE ANY MONEY! BESIDES, YOU COULD NEVER REACH THAT TREE!

HOW ABOUT THIS:

IF I HIT THAT TREE WITH **THIS** SNOWBALL, I GET TO HIT **YOU** WITH **ANOTHER** SNOWBALL!

FINE. YOU WON'T HIT THAT TREE IN A MILLION YEARS.

HERE GOES.

POW!

BY GOLLY, YOU'RE RIGHT! I WASN'T EVEN **CLOSE**!

big NATE
by Lincoln Peirce

Panel 1:
I WANT TO FIGURE OUT HOW TO DRAW CARICATURES.

I TOOK A CLASS ABOUT THAT ONCE! I'LL GIVE YOU SOME TIPS!

Panel 2:
ALL PEOPLE HAVE CERTAIN FEATURES THAT MAKE THEM STAND OUT! I'VE GOT A SQUARE HEAD AND A CROOKED NOSE! YOU'VE GOT SPIKY HAIR!

Panel 3:
AS A CARICATURIST, YOU TRY TO **EXAGGERATE** THOSE FEATURES!

SO IF SOMEONE HAS A BIG NOSE, YOU DRAW IT **HUGE!** GOTCHA!

Panel 4:
OOH! GORDIE! DRAW A CARICATURE OF ELLEN!

OKAY! WELL, OBVIOUSLY I'LL START WITH—

Panel 5:
!

Panel 6:
ACTUALLY, ELLEN'S FEATURES ARE SO FLAWLESS THAT A CARICATURE OF HER JUST WOULDN'T WORK.

Panel 7:
SEE YOU, NATE.

Panel 8:
NO SPINE

big NATE

by Lincoln Peirce

!

WHOA! **WHOA,** MR. EUSTIS! WHAT ARE YOU DOING?

I'M ABOUT TO SHOVEL MY DRIVEWAY.

SAVE YOURSELF THE LABOR, MR. EUSTIS! HIRE "N.F.T. YARDCARE"!

I'LL SHOVEL YOU OUT FOR TEN BUCKS!

THANKS, BUT NO, THANKS.

AW, HOW COME? WHY DO IT YOUR**SELF** WHEN **I'M** HERE?

AFTER ALL, YOU **HAVE** AVAILED YOURSELF OF MY SERVICES **BEFORE**!

YES, I KNOW.

FWOOSH!

AS I RECALL, I HIRED YOU TO RAKE MY LEAVES **THREE WEEKS AGO**!

YOU KNOW, YOU WERE NEXT ON MY LIST...

BIG NATE

by Lincoln Peirce

Howdy, friends! *BIFF BIFFWELL* here with another edition of...

WHAT'S YOUR JOB?

Here's our first guest, HOWARD PLOTZ! Tell us, Howard: "What's your job?"

Resolution accountant, Biff.

Hmm... What does that involve?

Well, Biff, at this time of the season, millions of people are making New Year's resolutions!

And you keep track of them?

Right! As you can see, my ledger has two columns: resolutions KEPT and resolutions BROKEN!

Seems like a pretty big job for one guy!

Oh, it is. I can't possibly keep up with the numbers by myself!

That's why I employ a world-wide network of helpers to act as my eyes and ears!

You have SPIES?

Hey, SOME-one's got to be there when a resolution gets broken!

AH HA!

OOPS

big NATE

by Lincoln Peirce

WELL? HOW'D IT GO?

GREAT!

I NAILED HIM POINT-BLANK WITH THREE SNOWBALLS!

HEE HEE!

THAT'LL TEACH NATE NOT TO CHALLENGE ME TO ANY MORE SNOWBALL FIGHTS!

HE HAS ABSOLUTELY **NO CLUE** ABOUT THE ART OF WAR!

HE HAS NO CUNNING! NO BATTLE INSTINCTS WHATSOEVER!

LIKE THE WAY I USED **YOU** AS A DOUBLE AGENT! SHEER GENIUS! YOU THINK **HE'D** EVER THINK UP A PLAN LIKE THAT?

I'M NOT SURE...

WHY DON'T YOU ASK HIM?

YAAAA

CLIK!

COCOA?

LOVE SOME!

by Lincoln Peirce

PASS! PASS!

WHUMP!

PTOO!

STOMP!!

!

zinnngg

oof!

grunt!

zinnggggg.

FWING!

SLUP!

SWISH!

JUST THE WAY I DIAGRAMED IT.

I GET AN ASSIST FOR THAT, RIGHT?

big NATE

by Lincoln Peirce

ALMANACS
1 ¢

♪

MAN, THAT SOCIAL STUDIES TEST WAS A **BREEZE**!

SOME OF THOSE QUESTIONS WERE SO **EASY**! WE'RE TALKING TOTAL SLAM DUNKS!

LIKE NUMBER FIVE, FOR EXAMPLE: "WHO PUBLISHED 'POOR RICHARD'S ALMANAC'?"

I MEAN... **DUH!** THAT'S LIKE "WHO'S BURIED IN GRANT'S TOMB?"

OBVIOUSLY THE PUBLISHER OF "POOR RICHARD'S ALMANAC" WAS **POOR RICHARD!**

WHAT DID HE MEAN, "POOR NATE"?

FIGURE IT OUT.

HEY, FRANCIS! GIVE ME A HAND!

WHAT ARE YOU DOING?

WHAT DOES IT **LOOK** LIKE? I'M PREPARING FOR THE MOTHER OF ALL SNOWBALL FIGHTS!

HELP ME BUILD UP MY SUPPLY OF AMMO!

OKAY!

THAT'S IT! KEEP MAKIN' 'EM! YOU CAN NEVER HAVE TOO MANY SNOWBALLS!

WHAT AN ARSENAL!

I THINK WE'RE READY TO START THE BATTLE!

SCOUT OUT THE AREA AND SEE IF YOU CAN SPOT THE ENEMY!

RIGHT!

?

SAY, WHO **IS** THE—?

POW!

TAP TAP TAP

FORT NATE

WHOA! WHOA! HALT!

WHAT'S **YOUR** PROBLEM?

YOU ARE MY PROBLEM! YOU AND YOUR **FIGURE SKATES!**

WE'RE PLAYING HOCKEY HERE, ELLEN! **HOCKEY!**

WE CAN'T HAVE YOU HACKING UP OUR RINK WITH YOUR LITTLE PICKS!

FIGURE SKATING IS AN **ABOMINATION!** IT'S AN INSULT TO ICE EVERYWHERE!

CAN ANYONE TELL ME WHY FIGURE SKATES WERE EVEN INVENTED IN THE **FIRST PLACE?**

POINK!

YOW OW OW OW!!

OOH! TRIPLE AXEL!

LOUSY FORM THOUGH.

big NATE by Lincoln Peirce

ZAP!

OKAY... MAGIC MOMENT COMING UP HERE...

JENNY'S MY PARTNER ON THIS SCIENCE PROJECT... OUR ARMS ARE ONLY INCHES APART...

ALL I NEED TO DO IS CASUALLY MOVE A BIT TO THE LEFT...

OUR HANDS WILL TOUCH... OUR EYES WILL MEET... DESTINY!!

OW!

POP!

WHOOPS... SORRY...

WHAT ARE YOU **DOING**, YOU IDIOT? YOU GAVE ME AN ELECTRIC **SHOCK!**

HEH HEH... I...UH... THAT IS...

?! YOU'RE **LAUGHING**?? YOU THINK THIS IS FUNNY? IS THIS **FUNNY** TO YOU?

POW!

WHAT'S WITH NATE'S HAIR?

MUST BE STATIC.

by Lincoln Peirce

OW!

note: in the back

HOLD IT, TEDDY!

WHOA! WHOA! WHAT ARE YOU DOING?

HAVING A SNOWBALL FIGHT WITH FRANCIS... AS IF YOU DIDN'T KNOW!

WHAT'S THAT SUPPOSED TO MEAN?

DON'T PLAY INNOCENT! I FELL FOR THAT LAST TIME!

OH. YOU MEAN WHEN I AMBUSHED YOU WHILE WORKING AS FRANCIS' DOUBLE AGENT?

DUH! YOU'RE OBVIOUSLY WORKING FOR HIM AGAIN!

YOU'RE JUST ASSUMING THAT! WHAT IF YOU'RE WRONG?

HUH?

HOW DO YOU KNOW I'M WORKING FOR FRANCIS? HOW DO YOU KNOW I'M NOT WORKING FOR YOU?

HMM... THAT'S RIGHT. MAYBE YOU ARE WORKING FOR ME...

HEY, BUT WAIT A MINUTE! IF YOU WERE WORKING FOR ME, WOULDN'T I—?

POW!

JUST FOR THE RECORD, I'M NOT WORKING FOR YOU.

CAN WE PLAY SOMETHING ELSE? THIS IS TOO EASY.

bIg NATE

by Lincoln Peirce

DAD? WILL YOU TELL ME THAT MOVIE STORY AGAIN?

WHAT MOVIE STORY?

YOU KNOW... ABOUT WHEN YOU WERE A KID... GOING TO THE MATINEE...

AH! YOU MEAN THE "CREATURE FEATURE"!

EVERY SATURDAY, MY BEST FRIEND JERRY PITTS AND I WOULD RIDE OUR BIKES DOWN TO THE OLD STRAND THEATRE!...

FOR **TWO BUCKS** YOU COULD WATCH A HORROR MOVIE, EAT A POPCORN AND DRINK A SODA! ALL WHILE SITTING IN THE **BALCONY**! THOSE WERE THE DAYS!

ALL THAT FOR TWO DOLLARS? YOWZA!

HARD TO BELIEVE, ISN'T IT?

BUT WHERE'D YOU GET THE MONEY?

FROM MY FATH—

...ER

THE MOVIE'S ON DAD, GRAMPS!

ABOUT TIME.

big NATE

by Lincoln Peirce

"BLAME PIE"

Pie chart segments: Poor coaching, Lame teammates, Fickle fans, Incompetent referees, Me

COME ON, 'CATS! PICK UP THE PACE!

YOU CUT TO THE LEFT! YOU WERE **SUPPOSED** TO CUT TO THE **RIGHT!**

HE FOULED ME! HE WAS ALL OVER ME!

COVER THAT GUY! **COVER** HIM!

WAKE UP, MARSHALL! PLAY YOUR POSITION!

BUZZZZZZ

ME?

WHY ARE YOU TAKING **ME** OUT? TAKE OUT ONE OF **THEM!**

HE'S REDEFINING THE ROLE OF "POINT" GUARD.

by Lincoln Peirce

BIG NATE by Lincoln Peirce

Test Your Knowledge! Test Your Skill!

TAKE THE...

Mrs. GODFREY "FUN FACTS" QUIZ!

1. Mrs. Godfrey became a social studies instructor because:

"You'll never amount to anything."

A. A career as a ballet dancer just didn't pan out.
B. She loves useless facts about obscure 16th century explorers.
C. She enjoys ~~warping~~ teaching young people.

2. Mrs. Godfrey's middle initial, B, stands for:

A. Beth
B. Barbara
C. Beelzebub

3. Mrs. Godfrey's favorite perfume is called:

"oolp! What a stench!"

A. "Charlie"
B. "Myron"
C. "Dead Fish"

4. Which of the following can be found in Mrs. Godfrey's desk:

"What are YOU looking at?"

A. Breath mints
B. "Sweatin' To The Oldies" tape
C. Magazine article entitled "Rodents: Our Misunderstood Cousins"

5. "1776" refers to:

A. The signing of The Declaration of Independence.
B. Washington crossing the Delaware.
C. Mrs. Godfrey's weight.

6. When not behind her desk, Mrs. Godfrey can be found:

DO NOT DISTURB

A. At the candy machine in the teachers' lounge.
B. Performing her twice-daily eyebrow trimming.
C. Under a nearby rock.

PERSONALLY, I'D PUT "C" FOR NUMBER SIX!

UH.... I'LL JUST PUT "NONE OF THE ABOVE."

big NATE

by Lincoln Peirce

OH, **NO!** WHAT'S **HE** DOING HERE?

THAT GUY? HE'S HERE TO TAKE PHOTOS!

YOU KNOW, ACTION SHOTS! DURING THE GAME!

AAARRGH! COULDN'T SOMEBODY **ELSE** DO IT? THAT GUY IS MY **NEMESIS!**

HE TAKES OUR CLASS PHOTOS EVERY YEAR AND ALWAYS CATCHES ME WITH THE **STUPIDEST** LOOK ON MY FACE!

THAT'S BECAUSE YOU'RE **POSING!** YOU'RE SELF-CONSCIOUS!

BUT YOU WON'T HAVE THAT PROBLEM DURING THE **GAME!** YOU'LL BE TOO BUSY **PLAYING!**

TWEET!

HMM.. YOU'RE RIGHT!

BZZZZZZZ TIME OUT, HOME TEAM!

WHEW! WATER!

HEY! MY RETAINER'S IN THERE!

PTOO!

KLIK!

65

by Lincoln Peirce

HUM HUMMM HUM DE DUM...

GOOD MORNING, MRS. GODFREY!

WHAT'S GOOD ABOUT IT, NATE?

I COMPLETED THE HOME-WORK, MA'AM!

GIVE ME THAT!

HMM... NATE, THIS IS EXTRAORDINARY WORK. BUT SINCE I DON'T LIKE YOU, I'M GIVING YOU A "D."

BUT THAT'S NOT FAIR!

ASK ME IF I CARE, KID! NYA HA HA HA HA HA!

MRS. GODFREY! LOOK OUT!

HMM?

WHAM!

OOPS.

...ASE ...ACK ...TRA ...Y!

NATE, ISN'T IT TIME FOR YOUR VISIT WITH THE SCHOOL COUNSELOR?

BIG NATE

by Lincoln Peirce

BRAVO!

6.0

AARRGH! FIGURE SKATING **AGAIN**?

YUP!

HOW CAN YOU WATCH THIS SCHLOCK?

IT'S NOT SCHLOCK! IT'S **EXCITING**!

AND IT'S **BEAUTIFUL**, TOO! LOOK AT TATIANA! SHE'S SO **GRACEFUL**!

GRACEFUL? SHE LOOKS LIKE SHE'S BEING ATTACKED BY HORNETS!

THAT'S CALLED **CHOREOGRAPHY**, IDIOT!

NICE **COSTUME**, TOO! WHAT DID SHE DO, ROLL AROUND ON THE FLOOR OF A SEQUIN FACTORY?

RRINNG!

HELLO?... OH, HI, FRANCIS... YUP, YOU CERTAINLY MAY SPEAK TO NATE.

LET ME GO GET HIM. HE'S WATCHING FIGURE SKATING.

NO!

OOP. HERE HE IS NOW.

BIG NATE

by Lincoln Peirce

Above... dove... glove... muv... nuv... puv... wuv...

※ AHEM ※

MY LOVE IS LIKE A RED, RED ROSE THAT BLOOMS WITH PETALS SWEET. MY LOVE, LIKE MOUNT ST. HELENS, GLOWS WITH AWE-INSPIRING HEAT.

MY LOVE IS LIKE A PERFECT PEARL PLUCKED FROM AN OYSTER PRIME. MY LOVE IS LIKE A FUZZY SQUIRREL (I HAD TO MAKE IT RHYME).

MY LOVE JUST CANNOT BE DENIED, CANNOT BE STOPPED OR SQUELCHED. IT'S LIKE A SIGH THAT MUST BE SIGHED, A BURP THAT MUST BE BELCHED.

YOU'VE DATED MANY OTHER GUYS. (EXCUSE ME WHILE I YAWN.) THEY'RE LIKE A BURGER, SHAKE AND FRIES, WHILE I'M FILET MIGNON.

UNTIL YOU STOP IGNORING ME, UNTIL WE HAVE A DATE, UNTIL TO LOVE ME YOU AGREE, I'M YOURS SINCERELY... NATE.

HEAR THAT, JENNY? THAT WAS FOR **YOU**!

OKAY, NOW FOR THIS MORNING'S ANNOUNCEMENTS...

big NATE
by Lincoln Peirce

PEACE QUIET

TEACHERS' LOUNGE! SEE THAT? **TEACHERS' LOUNGE!**

HOW COME **THEY** GET A ROOM TO HANG OUT IN AND **WE DON'T**?

WE'RE THE ONES WHO REALLY **NEED** A PLACE LIKE THAT! **WE'RE** THE ONES WHO ARE UNDER ALL THE **STRESS!**

WHILE THEY'RE IN THERE EATING DONUTS AND TAKING CATNAPS, WE'RE OUT HERE RUNNING AROUND LIKE RATS IN A MAZE!

IS IT ASKING TOO MUCH FOR US TO HAVE A PLACE FOR OURSELVES?...WHERE WE CAN **RELAX** FOR A CHANGE?

JUST GIVE US A **ROOM**, THAT'S ALL! I MEAN, DON'T WE **DESERVE** THAT? **DON'T WE??**

ALL I WANT IS A LITTLE PEACE AND~

QUIET PLEASE

DETENTION

big NATE

by Lincoln Peirce

FREEZE!

HA! NICE TRY, FRANCIS, BUT NO CIGAR!

FORT NATE

"FORT NATE" IS **IMPREGNABLE**!

FROM MY SPOT UP ON THIS HILL, I CAN REPEL **ANY** ATTACK!

FORT NATE

NOBODY CAN SNEAK UP ON ME! NOBODY CAN DEFEAT ME! I AM **INVINCIBLE**!

FORT NATE

I'LL TAKE ON ALL CHALLENGERS! "FORT NATE" WILL **NOT** BE CAPTURED!

FORT NATE

FORT NATE

TAP TAP

WATERLOO

big NATE

by Lincoln Peirce

WHAT'S NEW IN THE ART ROOM?

IT'S STILL LIFE WEEK!

WHY SO MANY?

BECAUSE I LET THE STUDENTS CREATE THEIR **OWN** STILL LIFES!

IT'S MUCH MORE INTERESTING THAN HAVING THEM PAINT STILL LIFES THAT **I** SET UP!

THIS WAY, THEY'RE PAINTING THINGS THAT ARE **SIGNIFICANT** TO THEM! THEY TAKE OWNERSHIP OF THEIR ARTWORK!

IT'S FUN FOR **ME**, TOO! I CAN LOOK AT THESE STILL LIFES AND TRY TO FIGURE OUT WHAT THESE KIDS ARE ALL ABOUT!

SOME OF THEM ARE EASIER TO DECODE THAN OTHERS.

COMIN' THROUGH! MY STILL LIFE NEEDS MORE CHEEZ DOODLES!

big NATE

by Lincoln Peirce

Time Once Again For The Adventures Of...

SUPERDAD!

...The world's **ONLY** bald super-hero with a slight paunch!

One day at **SUPERDAD'S** secret headquarters...

RRRRRINNNG!

EGAD! It's the HOTLINE!

What's that, Commissioner? You say it's **SNOWING** outside?

ZOUNDS! You're **RIGHT!**

This can only mean **ONE THING:** the **DRIVEWAY** needs to be **SHOVELED!**

DRAMATIC MUSIC

THIS is a job for...

Hmm... That looks like **wet** snow!... **Heavy** snow!

My back's been a little tender lately...

Plus, I've got this nasty hang-nail!

...But this shoveling **MUST** be done!

There's **GOT** to be a way!

73

big NATE

by Lincoln Peirce

Time Once Again, Friends, To Open...

Dan Cupid's **MAIL BAG!**

Hello again, gang! Today's first letter is from **NATE** and **ELLEN WRIGHT**, a brother and sister who ask: "Dan, please bring some **ROMANCE** into our father's life!"

At first, this seems like a SIMPLE REQUEST! **BUT...** watch what happens!

First, I shoot Nate and Ellen's Dad with one of my official **LOVE DARTS®**! He is now ready for love! He is **SUSCEPTIBLE!**

SPROING!

But when I search for a **MATE** for Dad, there's trouble! **WHY?** Because Dad has no **LIFE!** He never **GOES** anywhere!

It's hard to find someone to hook up with Dad when all he does is sit around the house!

The result: Dad, still under the spell of my **LOVE DART®**, now inappropriately transfers his affections **ELSEWHERE!**

ISN'T "THE NANNY" THE CUTEST THING?

SAD.

PATHETIC.

big NATE

by Lincoln Peirce

Letters! He gets Letters!

DAN CUPID'S VALENTINE MAILBAG!!

Well, friends, it's that time of year again, and the mail from lonely hearts has **REALLY** been piling up!

As the world's #1 matchmaker, I can say with confidence that I'll be able to find mates for **ALMOST** all these people!

Why "**ALMOST**," you ask? Simply put, there is a small group of folks out there with **NO CHANCE** of finding love!

example

Yes, it's tragic...but there **IS** something I can do!

Looove... Exciting and new...

Watch carefully as I aim two love darts: the first at the lonely person; and the second at...well... whatever's handy!

sproing! sproing!

It might not be true love between two human beings, but it's better than **NOTHING**!

BIG NATE

by Lincoln Peirce

 WHAT'S THAT FOR? / I'VE WRITTEN A VAL-ENTINE SONG FOR JENNY!

 I'M PULLING OUT ALL THE STOPS TO SHOW HER THAT SHE'S THE ONLY ONE FOR ME!

 ♪ OH JENNY... YOU'RE SO FIIINE! WILL YOU BE MY VALENTIIIINE?... / PLINK! PLUNK!

 OH WO JEN— ♪ / OOP! HI. / !

 JENNY AND HER FAMILY ARE OUT OF TOWN. / I'M HOUSE-SITTING. / OH. OKAY.

 DANG! SHE'S NOT HOME! / TOO BAD.

 YOUR SONG WILL GO TO WASTE. / OOH! HEY! YOU! WHAT'S YOUR NAME?

 YEAH, YOU! WHAT'S YOUR NAME? / PATTY

 ♪ OH PATTY... YOU'RE SO FIIINE!... / HE'S VERY ADAPTABLE.

BIG NATE

by Lincoln Peirce

Time Once Again FOR...

CELEBRITY INTERVIEW!

Here's your host: CHIP CHIPSON!

Greetings, friends! We're chatting with love-meister DAN CUPID about the yearly madness known as **SPRING FEVER!**

What's the word, Chip?

Let's start with the basics, Dan: **WHY** is **SPRING** known far and wide as the "season of love"?

CUPID TRAINING, Chip!

When Spring arrives, hundreds of apprentice cupids graduate from our "Love Academy" and begin their training period "in the field"!

This is the first time these trainees have had a chance to use actual "love darts" on real people!

As you might expect, they want to earn their stripes! So they shoot at anything that MOVES! Even if that target has **ALREADY BEEN HIT!**

But... doesn't that cause problems?

Well... yes, it **CAN** get ugly...

HIIIIII...

HI

HEY!

BIG NATE by Lincoln Peirce

1823 - Monroe ~~Dock~~ Doctrine
Pres. Monroe opposed to Euro
NATE!
Dr. Cesspool

MAJOR STUDY SESSION!

OKAY, HERE'S ANOTHER ONE:

BRIEFLY DESCRIBE WHAT THE "MONROE DOCTRINE" WAS.

HMMM... WELL, WHATEVER IT WAS, IT OBVIOUSLY INVOLVED SOME GUY NAMED MONROE...

MONROE **DOCTRINE**, YOU SAID? SO THAT MEANS HE WAS A **DOCTOR**, MAYBE... RIGHT? BUT I DON'T REMEMBER ANY DOCTORS IN MY CLASS NOTES...

BUT **SPEAKING** OF DOCTORS... (HEE HEE!)... WANNA SEE MY LATEST "DOCTOR CESSPOOL" COMIC? HE AMPUTATES THIS GUY'S FOOT, SEE, AND THEN... **OH!**

THAT REMINDS ME! DID YOU SEE JEFF BRINKER'S FOOT AFTER PHYS. ED ON FRIDAY? THE THING WAS THE SIZE OF A **BASKETBALL**! ALL SWOLLEN AND BRUISED AND—

WHAT WAS THE QUESTION?

HE USUALLY DOES BETTER WITH "MULTIPLE CHOICE."

big NATE

by Lincoln Peirce

SIXTY YEARS FROM NOW...

When did Ponce de Leon arrive in Florida?

Hey, ask me if I care!

OKAY, HERE'S MY POINT...

NOBODY EVER LOOKS BACK ON THEIR LIFE AND RE-GRETS THAT THEY DIDN'T DO MORE HOMEWORK!

DO OLD PEOPLE SIT AROUND SAYING, "GOSH, I WISH I'D DONE THAT SOCIAL STUDIES HOME-WORK SIXTY YEARS AGO"?

NO! THEY WISH THEY'D SPENT MORE TIME HAVING FUN! PLAYING! DOING STUFF THEY ACTUALLY LIKE TO DO!

I HAPPEN TO UNDERSTAND THAT! I'M NOT GOING TO FRITTER AWAY THE BEST YEARS OF MY LIFE HELD HOSTAGE BY SCHOOL!

HAND 'EM IN, PEOPLE.

TEMPUS FUGIT

DETENTION

big NATE by Lincoln Peirce

"SCHOOL DAYS"

P.S. 38
PARENTS NIGHT
6:00 – 8:00
WELCOME TO ALL!

ONE THING THAT ALWAYS SURPRISES ME IS HOW **LITTLE** PARENTS REALLY KNOW ABOUT THEIR CHILDREN'S SCHOOL LIVES!

SURE, YOU CAN ASK THEM "HOW WAS SCHOOL?" BUT WHAT DO YOU REALLY **LEARN?**

THAT'S WHY AN EVENING LIKE THIS CAN BE SO MUCH FUN!

YOU CAN SEE YOUR KIDS' CLASSROOMS! THEIR DESKS! EVEN THEIR **LOCKERS!**

OPENING YOUR CHILD'S LOCKER CAN INTRODUCE YOU TO A KID WHO'S **VERY DIFFERENT** FROM THE ONE YOU SEE AT HOME!

KSSSSSCCH!

...OR A KID WHO'S ALL TOO FAMILIAR.

big NATE

by Lincoln Peirce

SOMETHING'S NOT RIGHT HERE...

WHAT'S NOT RIGHT?

THIS COMIC STRIP I'M WORKING ON.

IT'S JUST NOT FUNNY! BUT ACCORDING TO ALL THE RULES OF CARTOONING, IT SHOULD BE HILARIOUS!

WHAT "RULES OF CARTOONING"?

THERE ARE CERTAIN THINGS THAT ARE SURE-FIRE LAUGH-GETTERS IN COMIC STRIPS! AND I'VE GOT ALL OF 'EM IN HERE!

I'VE GOT A MONKEY, A GUY SLIPPING ON A BANANA PEEL, A TALKING DUCK...

...A FAT GUY IN HIS UNDER-WEAR, A FALLING ANVIL, A HAIRLESS CAT, A GUY GETTING HIT IN THE FACE WITH A PIE...

...AND YET IT'S STILL KIND OF FLAT! I NEED MORE! I'VE GOT TO ADD SOME-THING ELSE!

HOW ABOUT A WEDGIE?

HEY! YEAH!

YANK!

THE GALLING THING IS THAT, TECHNICALLY, I GAVE HIM PER-MISSION TO DO THAT.

by Lincoln Peirce

HOME ←   SCHOOL →

≫ SIGH... ≫

WHAT'S WRONG, NATE?

THE **CONTRACT** MY DAD MADE ME SIGN, THAT'S WHAT'S WRONG! IT'S **KILLING** ME!

UNTIL I BRING MY GRADES UP, HE'S NOT LETTING ME DO **ANY-THING!**

NO CLUBS!... NO TEAMS!...NO EXTRA-CURRICULAR ACTIVITIES OF **ANY KIND!**

ALL OF A SUDDEN EVERYONE'S TEAS-ING ME AND SAY-ING I HAVE NO LIFE!

THE WHOLE SCHOOL'S LAUGHING AT ME! THEY CALL ME "STRAIGHT HOME" WRIGHT BECAUSE THAT'S WHERE I GO AFTER SCHOOL: **STRAIGHT HOME!**

WELL, SHAME ON THEM, THEN!

THE NUMBER OF **TEAMS** SOME-ONE'S ON ISN'T THE MEASURE OF A PERSON!

IT'S WHO YOU **ARE** THAT MATTERS, NOT WHAT YOU **DO!**

YOU ARE NOT WHAT YOU DO, NATE! OKAY? YOU ARE **NOT** WHAT YOU DO!

...OR SO I KEEP TELLING MYSELF.

OW! DANG!

AN APPLE FOR THE TEACHER?

YUP!

YOU SHOULD TRY IT! IT WOULDN'T HURT YOU TO GET ON HER GOOD SIDE!

NO, THANKS.

SUIT YOURSELF! **I'LL** GET ON HER GOOD SIDE!

YOU DO THAT.

MRS. GODFREY?

YES, FRANCIS?

I HAVE A LITTLE SOMETHING FOR YOU!

JUST A LITTLE TOKEN OF MY ESTEEM, THAT'S ALL!

CRUNCH!

THANKS FOR BEING A GREAT TEACHER!

WELL, ISN'T THAT—

!

I'M ASKING THE SCHOOL NURSE FOR A COPY OF YOUR DENTAL RECORDS.

big NATE by Lincoln Peirce

5th inning
JOE'S
4th inning
1st inning
3rd inning

WHAT A GAME! — IT WAS NICE TO ACTUALLY **WIN** ONE! — HMPH! SOME GAME!

I WALKED FOUR TIMES AND DIDN'T GET A SINGLE BALL HIT TO ME IN THE FIELD!

LOOK AT MY UNIFORM! NOT A SINGLE SMUDGE! NOT A SINGLE STAIN!

IF WE RUN INTO ANYONE WE KNOW, THEY'LL THINK I SPENT THE ENTIRE GAME ON THE **BENCH**!

I'VE GOT TO MESS UP MY UNIFORM SO THAT I LOOK LIKE A **BALLPLAYER**!

SPLURCH!

DO YOU THINK I WANT TO WALK AROUND LOOKING LIKE A **LOSER**?

ROLL ROLL

THE EVIDENCE CERTAINLY SUPPORTS THAT, YES.

HEL-LO!

BIG NATE

by Lincoln Peirce

WHEEL of RAGE

DENIAL · ANGER · FURY · BILE · IRRITATION · RESENTMENT · HATRED

Time Once Again For... "FEELINGS" with your host: DR. WARREN FUZZY!

Greetings, inner children!

Friends, as you all know, my mission is to HELP people!... ...And here's someone who really needs help: MRS. GODFREY!

OPEN UP to me, Mrs. Godfrey! Why do you look so ANGRY all the time?

Because I AM angry, you Brillo-headed nimrod!

And what do you think is at the ROOT of this anger?

Hey, if you looked like ME, wouldn't you be ticked off?

CRAK!

Mrs. Godfrey, all this bitterness is causing a profound SOUL SICKNESS in your inner spirit! We must HEAL it!

But how?

By EXPRESSING the anger! If you release your rage at regular intervals on a daily basis, it won't build up inside!

...So all I need to do is find someone to use as the TARGET of my anger!

Exactly! Let the healing begin!

BIG NATE

by Lincoln Peirce

Time Once Again For...

★ ★ ★ ★ ★ ★ ★

Celebrity

INTERVIEW!!

with your host:

BIFF BIFFWELL!

Folks, I'm talking to our old friend **HOPSY** the **EASTER BUNNY!** Hopsy, you look **EXHAUSTED!**

I am, Biff.

That's understandable, Hopsy... after all, you just delivered candy to millions of children throughout the world!

Not just children, Biff!

Huh?

Bringing candy to kids is the **EASY** part of my job!

The thing that **REALLY** wrinkles my cotton is making those gigantic deliveries to **PARENTS!**

You... you bring candy to PARENTS?

Well... I'm not supposed to talk about it... but **OF COURSE** I do!

...And I'm not talking just a few jelly beans, either! If the **KIDS** ever saw what their **PARENTS** are getting, we'd have a **RIOT** on our hands!

HEY!

by Lincoln Peirce

POP QUIZ, PEOPLE!

POP!

Hello again, friends! Investigative reporter **CHIP CHIPSON** here with another edition of...

BEHIND THE SCENES IN THE **TEACHERS' LOUNGE!**

I'm here in the teachers' inner sanctum at P.S. 38, where Social Studies instructor **Mrs. GODFREY** is GRADING TESTS!

Multiple choice, Mrs. G?

Essay tests, Chip.

Why essays? So that you can assess each student's writing skills, expressive capabilities and subject knowledge?

:Snicker: Chip, you're so naive.

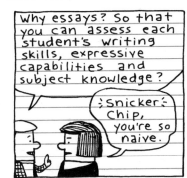

Essay tests are simply more **FUN** to grade! Why? Because there aren't any hard-and-fast "right" or "wrong" answers!

That enables me to indulge all my personal feelings about my students while assigning grades! Watch carefully...

Here's **NATE WRIGHT'S** essay! As we all know, I **DESPISE** Nate because his talent and charisma remind me what a miserable human being I am!

So you'll give him a bad grade? Even if his essay is **BRILLIANT**?

Precisely, Chip. Life's not fair. NYA HA HA HA!

D-MINUS?

JUST AN OBSERVATION: HIS FIRST NAME WAS "BENEDICT," NOT "TOM".

by Lincoln Peirce

GOOD GRAVY! **TIME OUT!**

THIS IS THE LAMEST PRACTICE WE'VE EVER HAD! WHAT'S **WITH** YOU GUYS?

YOU BIG GUYS ARE SUPPOSED TO BE OUR SCORING THREAT! YOU LOOK **PATHETIC** OUT THERE!

WE'RE GOING TO HAVE TO PLAY BETTER THAN THIS AGAINST JEFFERSON TOMORROW!

HOW, YOU ASK? I'LL TELL YOU! **I**, NATE WRIGHT, AM THE **KEY** TO THE GAME!

NONE OF **YOU** GUYS WANT TO TAKE CONTROL OF THIS TEAM, SO **I** WILL! CLIMB ON MY BACK!

YES, **I** WILL LEAD US TO VICTORY! I REPEAT: **CLIMB ON MY BACK!**

SOUNDS GOOD.

C-CAN'T BREATHE...

HEY, GUYS! HOP ON!

bIg NATE

by Lincoln Peirce

SUGAR PIE

CHATTER
CHATTER

GIGGLE YAK
YAK

OH, **THERE** YOU ARE, SUGAR PIE! I'VE BEEN LOOKING ALL OVER FOR YOU!

ER...I'LL SEE YOU LATER, JENNY.

seethe

LATER, BRAD!

NATE!

IN THE FLESH!

WILL YOU **STOP** DOING THAT!

DOING WHAT?

CALLING ME "SUGAR PIE"! I DON'T WANT TO BE CALLED THAT! YOU HAVE **NO RIGHT** TO CALL ME THAT!

HMMM... Y'KNOW, I SEE YOUR POINT...

IT'S NOT FAIR FOR ME TO GIVE **YOU** A PET NAME UNLESS YOU GIVE **ME** ONE!

WHY DON'T YOU CALL ME "CUDDLE BUNS"?

CUDDLE BUNS?!

I CAN'T TAKE IT.

WE'RE AN ITEM!

BIG NATE
by Lincoln Peirce

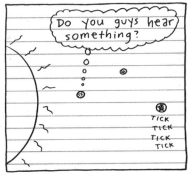

Do you guys hear something?

TICK
TICK
TICK
TICK

CARTOONING CLUB!

WOW!

MEETING TODAY

3:00   ROOM 115

DANG!

WHAT'S THE PROBLEM, TEDDY?

I'VE DRAWN MYSELF INTO A CORNER!

I DREW THE FIRST THREE PANELS OF A COMIC STRIP... AND NOW I DON'T KNOW HOW TO FINISH IT!

WRITER'S BLOCK, EH?

ALLOW **ME**, TEDDY! AS A FUTURE PROFESSIONAL CARTOONIST, I'M AN **EXPERT** AT THIS SORT OF THING!

HUMM DEE DUMM..... I'LL JUST ADD A FOURTH PANEL TO THE THREE YOU DID, AND... **VOILA**! A COMIC **MASTERPIECE**!

PANEL ONE: GUY WALKS INTO A PET STORE!...

PANEL TWO: GUY ASKS, "GOT ANY GOLDFISH?"

PANEL THREE: SALESMAN REPLIES, "I'M SORRY, SIR. NOT TODAY."

PANEL FOUR: PLANET EARTH, FOR NO APPARENT REASON, EXPLODES IN A FIERY BALL OF FLAME!

KA-BLOOM!

BY Lincoln Peirce

Biff Biffwell, "celebrity interviewer," speaks with...

APRIL SHOWERS!!

April, I think our viewers are wondering: what's happened to your usual **"SUNNY"** disposition?

Well, Biff, lately I...

SAAAAY! Who's **THAT**?

THAT'S the reason I'm in a bad mood: my obnoxious sister, **MAY FLOWERS**!

LOOK at her, will you? She thinks she's so great, tossing blossoms all over the place!

But who makes the flowers grow in the **FIRST** place? **ME**! I do all the work, **SHE** hogs all the credit!

Nobody **LIKES** rain, that's the problem! Nobody appreciates my talents! It's so **UNFAIR**!

Everyone's always asking, "why can't you be more like your sister?" I'm **SICK** of it!

ARE YOU TRYING TO MAKE A POINT HERE?

YOU'RE AN ONLY CHILD. YOU DON'T KNOW WHAT I'VE BEEN THROUGH.

CAN I HELP YOU?
I'M LOOKING FOR A MOTHER'S DAY CARD.

RIGHT OVER THERE. AISLE TWO.
I LOOKED AT THOSE AL- READY. I COULDN'T FIND WHAT I WAS LOOKING FOR.

DON'T YOU HAVE ANY THAT JUST SAY, "HAPPY MOTHER'S DAY, DAD"?

"HAPPY MOTHER'S DAY, **DAD**"?
YEAH.

WE DON'T HAVE ANY CARDS LIKE THAT...
HOW ABOUT ONE THAT SAYS, "DEAR DAD: SINCE MOM DIVORCED YOU, YOU'VE BEEN A GREAT MOTHER".

UH... NO.
HOW ABOUT "DAD: OTHER KIDS' MOMS AREN'T HALF THE MAN YOU ARE."

SORRY.

BERRYS STATIONERS "CARDS FOR ANY OCCASION"
HA!

by Lincoln Peirce

WHAM!

SPITSY! EASY! **DOWN**, BOY!

SLUP SLUP SLUP SLUP

SORRY ABOUT THAT, NATE.

※ SPLUT! ※ SPITSY, YOU **IDIOT!** WHAT IS **WITH** YOU?

PANT PANT PANT

WHAT'S WITH HIM? HE **MISSES** YOU, OF COURSE!

YOU TOOK CARE OF HIM ALL LAST WEEK! THE TWO OF YOU **BONDED!**

HE NOW THINKS OF YOU NOT JUST AS THE KID NEXT DOOR, BUT MORE LIKE A **PARENT!**

HAPPY MOTHER'S DAY!

big NATE

by Lincoln Peirce

KA CHINK!

KSSSCH!

RRRRUMBLE!..

? ?

RRRUMMBLE!..

FFFFOOOOOMM!

HI.

IT'S HIS END-OF-THE-YEAR LOCKER CLEANING.

by Lincoln Peirce

Panel 1: ALL RIGHT, "JOE'S CHICKEN"! LET'S LISTEN UP!

Panel 2: GUYS, THE SEASON'S NOT GOING WELL! WE'RE A LAUGHING-STOCK BECAUSE OF OUR RIDICULOUS TEAM NAME!

Panel 3: BUT TODAY WE CAN TURN IT ALL AROUND! WE CAN **BEAT** THIS TEAM AND START TO CHANGE EVERYONE'S OPINION OF US!

Panel 4: BUT TO DO THAT, WE'VE GOT TO FOCUS ON THE BASICS OF **BASEBALL**! PITCHING! HITTING! BASERUNNING! STRATEGY!

Panel 5: LET'S IGNORE ALL THE LAME JOKES AND WISE-CRACKS AND COME UP WITH A GAME PLAN! HOW ABOUT IT, "JOE'S CHICKEN"?

Panel 6: I THINK WE SHOULD JUST "WING" IT.

Panel 7: HEH HEH "WING" IT!... HA HA HA GOOD ONE, MAN! HEE HEE HA HA

Panel 8: HA HA HA HA HA HA HA HA HA HA HA HA — WE HEREBY FORFEIT DUE TO A LACK OF SELF-RESPECT.

BIG NATE

BY Lincoln Peirce

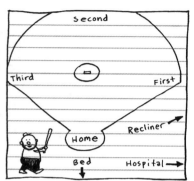

Diagram showing baseball field with labels: Second, Third, First, Home, Recliner, Bed, Hospital

HEY HEY HEY!

WANNA PLAY SOME CATCH?

SURE! I'LL GET MY GLOVE!

FINALLY IT'S REALLY STARTING TO FEEL LIKE **SPRING**!

THIS IS JUST THE SORT OF WEATHER THAT GETS ME PUMPED FOR BASEBALL!

THE SMELL OF THE GRASS... THE FEEL OF THE GLOVE...

THE ROAR OF THE CROWD...

THE CRACK OF THE BACK...

OF THE **BAT**, YOU MEAN.

NOPE. LOOK.

OH.

LAST YEAR, HE WAS IN TRACTION FOR TWO WEEKS.

BIG NATE

by Lincoln Peirce

Hey, TRIVIA LOVERS!!

Test your knowledge of everyone's favorite bleached-blonde high school sophomore!

⍰⍰⍰⍰⍰⍰⍰

TAKE THE Ellen Wright **FUN FACTS QUIZ!**

QUESTION 1: Ellen's IQ is less than that of:

What the...?

Ⓐ Her brother Nate
Ⓑ A sickly kitten
Ⓒ A potato
Ⓓ All of the above

Question 2: Ellen's boyfriend Gordie is:

Ⓐ A gentleman
Ⓑ A scholar
Ⓒ Woefully misguided
Ⓓ Insane

QUESTION 3: Ellen's hobbies include:

Ⓐ Mustache-bleaching
Ⓑ Quantum astrophysics
Ⓒ Sobbing in front of mirror
Ⓓ A and C

QUESTION 4: Ellen's reason for living is:

Move. SHOVE!
Oh, Billy.

Ⓐ Promoting world peace
Ⓑ Ending poverty
Ⓒ Achieving enlightenment
Ⓓ "Melrose Place"

Question 5: Which "clique" does Ellen belong to at school?

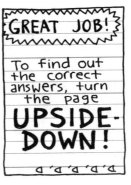

Hi, gang! | Who are you?

Ⓐ The "Preps"
Ⓑ The "Brains"
Ⓒ The "Jocks"
Ⓓ The "Friendless Losers"

GREAT JOB!

To find out the correct answers, turn the page **UPSIDE-DOWN!**

ᗡ ᗡ ᗡ ᗡ ᗡ

---

big NATE

by Lincoln Peirce

SO JENNY'S GOING STEADY WITH RONNIE DWYER! POOR NATE MUST BE **DEVASTATED!**

HE'LL LIVE

WHAT KIND OF ATTITUDE IS **THAT**, FRANCIS? NATE NEEDS OUR **SUPPORT!** HE'S PROBABLY REALLY HURTING!

I'M GONNA TALK TO HIM!

NATE? I...UH...I HEARD ABOUT JENNY AND RONNIE, AND... WELL, I JUST WANT TO SAY: I'M HERE FOR YOU!

I MEAN...THERE MUST BE A LOT GOING ON INSIDE YOU!...EATING AWAY AT YOU!

DON'T YOU THINK YOU'D FEEL BETTER IF YOU JUST...LET IT OUT?

LET WHAT OUT?

WHATEVER YOU'RE FEELING! DON'T THINK ABOUT IT! JUST LET IT OUT!

LET IT OUT. WELL... OKAY

BURRP!

HE'LL LIVE

YOU KNOW, I **DO** FEEL BETTER!

big NATE

by Lincoln Peirce

Hey! You're a beautiful crowd! I MEAN that!

Here's a li'l tune called: "The Alien & Sedition Acts of 1798"!

OH, HOW I HATE SOCIAL STUDIES. THIS FINAL EXAM IS GOING TO BE **BRUTAL**!

YOU'VE GOT TO FIND WAYS TO MAKE STUDYING **FUN**!

"FUN." RIGHT.

DO WHAT **I** DO! MAKE UP LITTLE POEMS ABOUT THE STUFF YOU'RE STUDYING!

LIKE THIS: "LEWIS AND CLARK IN 1804 WENT WAY OUT WEST TO CHART AND EXPLORE"!

HERE'S ANOTHER ONE: "ROBERT FULTON HAD A DREAM: TO SAIL A SHIP THAT RAN ON STEAM"!

HEY, THAT'S PRETTY GOOD!

AND IT **WORKS**, TOO! IT REALLY HELPS YOU REMEMBER THE STUFF!

❊CHUCKLE!❊ I COULDN'T HELP OVERHEARING! THAT'S A GOOD IDEA, FRANCIS!

...BUT YOU KNOW WHAT MIGHT WORK EVEN **BETTER**? SETTING THOSE POEMS TO **MUSIC**!

JOIN IN, BOYS!

PLINK PL NK

MAKING UP POEMS: GOOD ONE, BUDDY.

LET'S FIND SOMEWHERE ELSE TO STUDY.

BIG NATE

by Lincoln Peirce

"END O' SCHOOL" (a poem)

by Nate Wright

September brought us back to school,
A situation downright cruel.
And by October, we'd recalled,
Why by our school we're so appalled.

Here's tonight's homework.

Did I mention that homework counts for 80% of your grade?

GROOANNN

Dang!

November: time for Giving thanks.
I tried, but kept on Drawing blanks.

Thank goodness you didn't get an **F-MINUS**!

Shut up, man.

We reached December,
Inch by inch.
That Mrs. Godfrey:
What a grinch.

Our January resolution:
Start a 6th-grade revolution!

FOOD FIGHT!

February's short,
You mention?
Not if you spend it
In detention.

sigh...

tick tick tick

10

March and April came and went.
Can't we give up school for Lent?
May and June: we got exam'd.
I failed despite how much I crammed.

Ready for your test on Chapter Six?

But you told us to study Chapter **FIVE**!!

I changed my mind.

Now finally it's
Really summer!
School's out! Let's get...

"DUMB AND DUMBER"?

NAH. HOW 'BOUT "MEN IN BLACK"?

---

big NATE

by Lincoln Peirce

TIE GAME...

BOTTOM OF THE NINTH...

TWO OUTS...

BASES LOADED...

YES, IT'S DEFINITELY "CRUNCH" TIME!

CRUNCH!

OUR NEW RIGHT FIELDER IS EATING CHIPS.

COACH

big NATE

by Lincoln Peirce

BEEP
BEEP
BOOP
BEEP
BEEP
BOOP
BOOP

busy signal

BEEP
BEEP
BOOP
BEEP
BEEP
BOOP
BOOP

busy signal   busy signal

YAWN

BEEP
BEEP
BOOP
BEEP
BOOP
BOOP

busy signal

BEEP
BEEP
BOOP
BEEP
BEEP
BOOP
BOOP

RRRINNNG!

WKQC-FM! YOU'RE THE HUNDREDTH CALLER! WANT TO WIN A HUNDRED DOLLARS?

YES! YES!

OKAY, JUST ANSWER THIS QUESTION: WHO WAS FRANKLIN ROOSEVELT'S **FIRST** VICE PRESIDENT?

KLIK

THE "REDIAL" BUTTON CAN TAKE YOU TO THE STATION, BUT IT CAN'T GET YOU ON THE TRAIN.

big NATE

by Lincoln Peirce

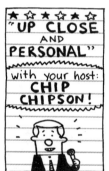

★★★★★★★ "UP CLOSE AND PERSONAL"

with your host: CHIP CHIPSON!

Hello again, friends! My special guest today: consumer reporter **CELINE PAYCHEK!**

Hi, Chip!

Celine, at this time of year, kids everywhere are wondering: WHAT can I get Dad for **FATHER'S DAY??**

I can help, Chip!

I've got plenty of gift ideas for the Dad who has everything!

For example: the **NOSTRIL PILOT,®** a handy little nose-hair trimmer!

BZZZZZZ

Or how about the **PANTS-HORN®** to help Dad into those slacks that have gotten ☆chuckle!☆ a bit snug!

HERE's a handy little item! An edible couch! No more pesky trips to the fridge during that big game!

AND it comes in chocolate, beef, and monterey jack!

YUM!

But Celine... what if a kid spent all his money on candy and video games, and can't **AFFORD** one of these gifts?

No problem at all, Chip!

Just dust off the ol' "it's the thought that counts" excuse! Give Dad something **HOMEMADE,** like a lame DRAWING you were planning to throw away ANYWAY! He'll **LOVE** it!

I LOVE IT!

☆PHEW!☆

BIG NATE

BY Lincoln Peirce

The SOUNDS of BASE-BALL

SCUFF SCUFF

TAP TAP

grunt!

KRAK!

CLAP CLAP CLAP CLAP CLAP

YAWNNN

ding ding ♫

THUMP!

ICE

WAP!

COACH

BY Lincoln Peirce

IN HONOR OF "CARTOON APPRECIATION WEEK," I'M GOING TO DO A LITTLE DEMONSTRATION!

I'LL START OFF WITH A SIMPLE DRAWING OF MY SISTER ELLEN!

NOW OBSERVE AS I USE A FEW CARTOONING TRICKS TO COMPLETELY CHANGE HER APPEARANCE!

FIRST I'LL ADD SOME EYEBROWS AND TEETH...

NEXT, I'LL MAKE HER FACE ALL FLUSHED...

...AND I'LL ADD STEAM COMING OUT OF HER EARS!

SWEAT BEADS ARE GOOD! AND I'LL CHANGE HER EYES A BIT!

HOW 'BOUT HER EYES SHOOTING DAGGERS?

AND... UH OH! SHE'S THINKING NASTY THOUGHTS!

SEE HOW EASY IT IS TO MAKE HER MAD?

GOOD THING IT'S JUST A CARTOON!

big NATE

by Lincoln Peirce

♡ oh, Nate! Seeing you hit that home run off my current boyfriend Ronnie has made me change my mind and fall madly in love with YOU! ♡

voice of Jenny →

KRAK!

WELL, WELL, **WELL!** LOOK WHO'S **PITCHING!**

RONNIE DWYER! THE ALL-AMERICAN BOY!

WHAT DOES JENNY **SEE** IN THIS GUY? HE'S SUCH A **JERK!**

BALL **ONE!**

BALL **TWO!**

BALL **THREE!**

HA! NOT ONLY IS HE A **JERK,** HE'S **AFRAID** OF ME! HE'S PITCHING **AROUND** ME!

WHATSA MATTER, RONNIE? AFRAID I'M GONNA PUT ONE OVER THE FENCE??

GIMME ALL YOU GOT, WIMP! COME ON! COME RIGHT AT ME!

WUMP!

WAS THAT REALLY CALLED FOR?

PRETTY MUCH WORD FOR WORD.

big NATE

by Lincoln Peirce

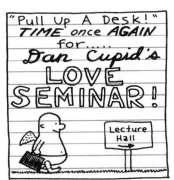

"Pull Up A Desk!" *TIME* once *AGAIN* for..... Dan Cupid's LOVE SEMINAR!

Lecture Hall

Recruits, I'm here to tell you that being a matchmaker isn't all flowers and valentines! It can be a tough business!

Take **THIS** time of year, for instance! We're coming face-to-face with the phenomenon called "**SUMMER LOVIN'**"!

Travolta   New John

"What's wrong with summer romance?" you ask? **EVERYTHING**!! It wipes out all of **OUR** hard work!

All year long we bust our humps bringing people together! We TIRELESSLY pair folks up and help them get through the long, cold winter!

But then **SUMMER** comes along! People get crazy! Blood runs hot!

Before you know it, some mindless summer flirtation can destroy the romances that **WE** worked so hard to create!

AHEM!

HI!

by Lincoln Peirce

AAAAHHH...

?

!

GAH!!

C-C-COLD...
S-SO
C-COLD...

IT'S USUALLY MID-JULY BEFORE THE NIGHTMARES STOP.

x

ErrorPUBLIC BEACH ALL WELCOME

116

BIG NATE

by Lincoln Peirce

Time For Another Edition Of...

UP CLOSE AND PERSONAL!

with your host: **BIFF BIFFWELL!**

Greetings, friends! Since today is Independence Day, it's a very appropriate time to chat with everyone's favorite relative... **UNCLE SAM!**

Yo, Biff. What it is!

Many folks probably don't know that the name "Uncle Sam" is an extension of the initials **U.S.!**

Righto, Biff! I'm one patriotic dude!

And RECOGNIZABLE, too! **EVERYONE** knows Uncle Sam!

Hey, when you dress like this, you can't be anonymous!

So you like the attention, then?

Oh, yeah! What's not to like?

Especially **TODAY!** The 4TH of July is the highlight of my entire **YEAR!**

It's a great feeling to know that at picnics and parades all over the country, people are going to be paying tribute to me however they can!

HEY, JENNY! "I WANT YOU"! HA HA! GET IT?

⌗SIGH...⌗

4TH OF JU
SCOUT TRO

BIG NATE

by Lincoln Peirce

WILBURN CHESS CAMP

NO TRESPASSING

ANOTHER MATCH?

NO, LET'S PLAY THE "SCRIBBLE GAME". I NEED TO THINK ABOUT SOMETHING BESIDES CHESS!

WHAT'S THE "SCRIBBLE GAME"?

I CLOSE MY EYES AND MAKE A QUICK SCRIBBLE, SEE...

THEN YOU HAVE TO TURN IT INTO SOMETHING!

THAT'S EASY! IT'S A CHESS BOARD!

draw draw

OKAY, THEN...TRY **THIS** ONE!

Scribble Scribble

THIS ONE'S OBVIOUS! IT'S A KNIGHT CAPTURING A ROOK!

draw draw

ALL RIGHT, DEREK... GET A LOAD OF **THIS** ONE!

scribble scrawl

LOOKS LIKE A DUCK PLAYING CHESS!

NO! **NO!** IT'S **NOT** A DUCK PLAYING CHESS! NOT **EVERYTHING** IS ABOUT **CHESS!**

YOU! KID! DOES THIS SCRIBBLE LOOK LIKE A DUCK PLAYING CHESS?

A DUCK PLAYING CHESS? NO...

IT'S A **MONKEY** PLAYING CHESS!

OOOH! YOU'RE **RIGHT!**

THEY'RE SCARING ME.

BIG NATE
by Lincoln Peirce

hands tied behind back
blindfolded
YOWZA!
CHECK-MATE!

HI, NATE!

HE CAN'T SPEAK TO YOU, DEREK.

YOUR BLABBERMOUTH PAL HERE WAS **YAKKING** SO MUCH, I MADE HIM PROMISE TO SHUT UP FOR THE REST OF THE MATCH!

WITHOUT THE ANNOYING SOUND OF HIS VOICE, I CAN CONCENTRATE ON **DESTROYING** HIM!

S I L E N C E

HA! **CHECK!** WHAT DO YOU SAY TO **THAT**, BIG MOUTH?

whisper whisper

HE SAYS "CHECKMATE."

WHA-? **WHAT?!**

HE ALSO SAYS "IN YOUR FACE."

big NATE

by Lincoln Peirce

SURE YOU WANT TO DO THAT?

OH, NO YOU DON'T, NATE! **NO YOU DON'T!**

WHAT?

YOU'RE TRYING TO GET ME TO TAKE BACK THAT MOVE!

I'VE GOT YOU ON THE ROPES, SO YOU'RE TRYING TO SOW THE SEEDS OF DOUBT IN MY MIND!

YOU ASK "SURE YOU WANT TO DO THAT?"... AS IF YOU'RE TRYING TO BE **HELPFUL**! HA!

WELL, I'VE BEEN PLAYING AGAINST YOU FOR **THREE WEEKS** NOW, NATE! I KNOW ALL YOUR TRICKS!

SO YES! **YES,** I'M SURE I WANT TO DO THAT!

CHECKMATE.

BUT... I THOUGHT YOU WERE USING REVERSE PSYCHOLOGY!

I WAS!

by Lincoln Peirce

HEY, LET'S PLAY BALL!

I GOTTA FINISH MOWING MR. STACK'S LAWN.

I'LL BE DONE IN FIVE MINUTES!

OKAY! I'LL WAIT!

PRRRRR

UH-OH...

THUMP! RRRRRRRRRRR

KACHUNK!

ZING!

CRASH!

TINKLE TINKLE

WHEN HE PAYS YOU, SEE IF YOU CAN GET MY BALL BACK...

big NATE

by Lincoln Peirce

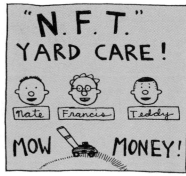

"N.F.T." YARD CARE!

Nate   Francis   Teddy

MOW   MONEY!

LET ME HANDLE THIS ONE!

DING DONG!

HI, MA'AM! I COULDN'T HELP NOTICING THAT YOUR LAWN NEEDS MOWING!

MY FRIENDS OVER THERE AND I HAVE A THRIVING LAWN CARE BUSINESS! MOWING, RAKING... WHATEVER!

IF YOU'D LIKE YOUR LAWN TO BE THE ENVY OF THE NEIGHBORHOOD, WE'RE YOUR MEN!

HERE'S OUR CARD! N.F.T. YARD CARE! REMEMBER THE NAME!

!! N.F.T. YARD CARE?

YOU'VE HEARD OF US, EH?

WHO HASN'T?

SLAM!

THE WHOLE "WORD OF MOUTH" THING MAY HAVE STARTED TO BOOMERANG ON US.

by Lincoln Peirce

GORDIE! WHAT'S WITH THE BIG MESS!?

INVENTORY! I'VE GOT TO ACCOUNT FOR EVERY ITEM IN THE STORE!

WHA–?... HEY, WHAT'S **THIS** DOING IN A **GARBAGE CAN**?

HM?... OH, WE'RE THROWING THAT OUT. YOU CAN TAKE IT IF YOU WANT.

REALLY?

IT'S ALL YOURS.

TEDDY!

CHECK OUT WHAT THEY WERE THROWING AWAY AT "KLASSIC KOMIX"!

WOW! CAPTAIN PICARD! HOW'D YOU–?

KRAK!

BIFF!

"HEADS UP"!

ALAS, POOR JEAN-LUC.

by Lincoln Peirce

NATE! IS THAT YOUR DOG?

WHO, **SPITSY**? HECK, **NO**! HE'S MY NEIGHBOR'S!

DO YOU HONESTLY THINK I'D OWN A DUMB DOG LIKE **THIS**? HE'D CHEW HIS OWN **PAWS** OFF IF YOU LET HIM!

THAT'S WHY HE WEARS THIS IDIOTIC **COLLAR**! TO PROTECT HIM FROM HIMSELF!

I MEAN, **LOOK** AT HIM IN THAT THING! HE LOOKS LIKE A **CLOWN**!

IF I WERE A DOG, I'D BE **EMBARRASSED** TO BE SEEN IN A COLLAR LIKE—

YANK!

OOF! OW! GAK!

BIG NATE

by Lincoln Peirce

His   Hers

GREETINGS, teen-age boys! Doctor **WARREN FUZZY** here, urging you to take a close look at your relationship and ask yourself the burning question:

WHO WEARS the PANTS: HER OR ME??

Select the response that most applies to **YOU!**

1.) During TV time with my girlfriend, we usually end up watching:

Richard! How COULD you? — SOB!

Ⓐ Something I like
Ⓑ Something we both like
Ⓒ "Caroline In The City"

2.) Some nights I wake up screaming because I was dreaming about:

YAIEE! NO! NO!

Ⓐ drowning in quicksand
Ⓑ falling off a cliff
Ⓒ my girlfriend going public with the fact that she calls me "pookie bear"

3.) When I take my girlfriend to a restaurant, I order:

Ooh! That looks yummy!

Ⓐ whatever I want
Ⓑ what I can afford
Ⓒ whatever my girlfriend suggests, then let her eat off my plate

4.) My most frequently-worn item of clothing is:

Ⓐ my letterman's jacket
Ⓑ my favorite jeans
Ⓒ a lavender cardigan my girlfriend gave me for our 3½-month anniversary

5.) When I pick up my girlfriend for a date, I bring with me:

sigh... — tick tick tick

Ⓐ flowers
Ⓑ candy
Ⓒ a magazine to read while waiting for her to get ready

HOW LONG DOES IT TAKE JUST TO PUT ON A DRESS?

ACTUALLY, I THINK SHE'S WEARING THE PANTS.

BIG NATE by Lincoln Peirce

WHO ARE WE PLAYING TODAY?

THE BULL-DOGS.

YYYESSS! THE BULLDOGS **STINK**! THEY'RE THE ONLY TEAM IN THE LEAGUE WITH A WORSE RECORD THAN **OURS**!

FOR ONCE, WHEN "JOE'S CHICKEN" TAKES THE FIELD, **WE'LL** BE THE FAVORED TEAM!

FOR ONCE, WE WON'T HAVE TO LISTEN TO THE OTHER TEAM **LAUGHING** AT US! THEY'LL KNOW THAT **WE** ARE A BETTER TEAM THAN **THEY** ARE!

I'VE ALMOST FORGOTTEN WHAT IT'S LIKE TO SEE **FEAR** IN AN OPPONENT'S EYES!

HEY, GUYS! LOOK WHO'S HERE!

IT'S "JOE'S CHICKEN"!

CLUCK! CLUCK!

HEH HEH!
BUCK BUCK BUH-**GAWK**!
HA HA HA HA HA
CLUCK CLUCK BUCK BUH-**GAW**!

BUCK BUCK HEE HEE BUH-**GAWK**! CLUCK CLUCK HA HA BUCK BUCK CLUCK CLUCK HA HA HA HA

I'VE COM**PLETELY** FORGOTTEN.

HEY, HEY! LET'S HIT THE ARCADE!

WHAT'S THAT FOR?

THIS IS MY **CARTOONIST'S NOTEBOOK!** I TAKE IT WITH ME WHEREVER I GO!

WHY, YOU ASK? SO WHEN I SEE SOMETHING FUNNY HAPPEN, I CAN QUICKLY WRITE IT DOWN TO USE LATER IN A CARTOON!

THERE'S NOTHING A CARTOONIST HATES MORE THAN FORGETTING A GOOD IDEA! THIS WAY, I FORGET **NOTHING!**

NYAAAAAA

WO WO WOW

bump bump bump bump

GAAAAA

TONK!

RRRRIP

SPLAT!

WANT ME TO WRITE THAT DOWN FOR YOU?

FORGET IT.

BALL FOUR!

OKAY, HERE WE GO! RALLY TIME! LATE INNING LIGHTNING!

LET'S SEE WHAT SIGNS COACH IS GIVING ME... HMMMM...

TWO TUGS AT HIS CAP... TWO TAPS ON HIS ARM...

WAIT A SEC... THAT WAS **THREE** TAPS... IS THAT THE "STEAL" SIGN?... HMM...

TWO HANDS ON HIS HIPS... ONE... NO, **TWO** CLAPS...

NOW ANOTHER CLAP... AND TWO TAPS ON HIS SHOULDER... WHAT DOES **THAT** MEAN?... THREE TAPS... TWO TUGS...

FOUR CLAPS... TWO SCRATCHES... THREE WHISTLES... ONE... TWO AAARRRGH!

SMAK!

yer OUT! TAG!

OKAY, HOW MANY FINGERS?

SHUT UP.

JENNY! I GOT YOU A TREAT FROM THE SNACK BAR!

WHO ASKED YOU TO GET ME A TREAT?

NOBODY! I WAS JUST BEING NICE!

WELL, I'M NOT EVEN HUNGRY, SO WHY—

HEADS UP!

ZING!

SLUP!

YOW! DID YOU SEE THAT, JENNY? THAT FRISBEE ALMOST—

NYAA!

WHAT? WHAT'S WRONG?

YOU DROPPED IT DOWN MY BACK!!

IT'S FREEZING! IT'S FREEZ-ING!!

I'LL GET IT! I'LL GET IT!

WHAT ARE YOU DOING? GET YOUR HANDS OUT OF MY SUIT!

I'M... I'M JUST... I WAS ONLY...

POW!

I HAVE A POPSICLE HEADACHE.

Time For...
Biff and *Chip...*

ON SAFARI!

G'day, mates!

Friends, we're here in suburbia to hunt for... the **TEEN-AGER** in her natural habitat!

Her scientific name is "BLEACHED BLONDIUS SELF-ABSORBIA"!

E-GADS, Biff! There she is!!

wipe wipe
spritz spritz
puff puff

What on Earth is she doing, Chip?

It's a bizarre grooming ritual, Biff! It's called "applying makeup"!

KLIK KLIK

Now she's looking in a mirror...

That's typical of the species, Biff! She **NEVER** tires of gazing adoringly at her own reflection!

tra la la

Hel-LO!

Why is she **ALONE**, Chip? Don't teen-agers travel in packs?

Not THIS teen, Biff! She's an **OUTCAST**, rejected by her peers! She's what we in the safari biz refer to as... a "LOSER!"

Careful with that dart gun!

I hear you, my friend! There are few things more TER-RIFYING than an angry teen-ager!

POP! - - - - -

A direct hit! But... OH, **NO!**

The sedative isn't working! She's going to charge! RUN!

WOO HOO HOO HOO

Peirce

131

big NATE

by Lincoln Peirce

 MY CAT-LIKE REFLEXES MAKE ME THE IDEAL CENTER FIELDER!

 THE INSTANT I HEAR THE CRACK OF THE BAT, I MOVE! MOVE! MOVE!

 BE ALERT, NOW... BE READY...

 CRACK!

 BACK BACK BACK BACK BACK BACK BACK BACK BACK

 YES, REFLEXES! THE MOST VITAL PART OF BEING A CENTER FIELDER!...

 WUMP!

 ...THOUGH DEPTH PERCEPTION IS KEY, TOO...

by Lincoln Peirce

sigh...

AARRGH

JAB!

NEW KITE?

SORT OF.

by Lincoln Peirce

BY Lincoln Peirce

BAM! BAM! BAM!

Time For Another Edition Of...
"WOW! WHAT A MAKEOVER!"

'Allo.

...with *INTERNATIONALLY ACCLAIMED* STYLIST...
MR. PIERRE!

Friends, today I will be attempting my most challenging makeover EVER: 15-year-old **ELLEN WRIGHT**!

¿Giggle! Bone joor, Mister Pierre!

Ellen, when I look at you, I clearly see you are a "WINTER" person!

Because I look good in blues and grays?

No, because you should stay indoors.

Let me first apply some "concealer" to your enormous nose...

Sacre bleu! It is not working!

Well then, perhaps I can add some color to your pasty-white, acne-scarred cheeks!

Egad! This makes it WORSE!

...And your coarse, lifeless hair resists even my best conditioner!

¿Sob! Oh, Mr. Pierre! Can't you help me?

I am sorry, my ugly little duckling. It is beyond even Mr. Pierre's powers.

If you want to change your appearance, you will have to do it on your own, at home.

ANY DAY NOW!

SHUT UP!

BIG NATE

by Lincoln Peirce

SOFA | COFFEE TABLE | CHAIR | CHAIR

TAP TAP TAP

JAM WAR

NATE...

HOLD IT, DAD! I ALREADY KNOW WHAT YOU'RE GOING TO SAY!

JAM-BO-REE

YOU DON'T WANT ME HANGING MY HOOP HERE! BUT I'VE GIVEN THIS A LOT OF THOUGHT!

THIS IS THE PERFECT LOCATION! IT'S NOT CLOSE TO ANY FURNITURE! IT'S NOT IN THE WAY OF ANYTHING!

PLUS, FEEL THE BALL! IT'S **FOAM**! IT WON'T BREAK THE LAMPS! IT WON'T CRACK THE PLASTER!

THERE'S ABSOLUTELY NO REASON NOT TO HAVE A HOOP HERE! OKAY, DAD? OKAY?

FINE, NATE. I HAVE NO OBJECTION TO HAVING THE HOOP HERE.

YES!

I WOULD, HOWEVER, LIKE TO DISCUSS THE 3-POINT LINE ON THE KITCHEN FLOOR.

WATCH IT, WATCH IT! THAT'S STILL WET!

big NATE

by Lincoln Peirce

Hello, sports fans! **BIFF** and **CHIP** here again to bring you...

18

A **"SLICE" OF LIFE!**

WIFF!

The Golfing Misadventures of **DAD!**

Here's Dad loosening up on the first tee!

When things get loose, Biff, they often fall apart COMPLETELY!

His swing reminds me of **BOBBY JONES!**

But... Bobby Jones is **DEAD!**

Exactly.

LURCH

HACK

Say, he got a lot of height on **THAT** shot!

Yes, he did... Unfortunately, he was **PUTTING** at the time!

They say golf is a game of inches, Chip!

In Dad's case, a whole **LOT** of them!

narf narf

42"

HOT DOGS

Okay, QUIET, everyone! Dad is preparing to hit!

Why are we whispering?

WOW! He... he **HIT** it!

This is AMAZING! Dad's ball is actually in the **FAIRWAY!**

WRONG FAIRWAY, DAD.

COULD YOU GO GET THAT ONE, SON?

BIG NATE

by Lincoln Peirce

BIG NATE
by Lincoln Peirce

Oh, Diary! I have SO MUCH to tell you!

Dang. Not again!

HI, NATE. IS ELLEN AROUND?

GORDIE! MY MAN! COME ON IN!

ELLEN'S UPSTAIRS. WHILE YOU WAIT, CAN I INTEREST YOU IN A LITTLE LIGHT READING?

LIGHT READING?

YUP! THIS HERE'S A HOT LITTLE PAGE-TURNER ENTITLED "ELLEN'S DIARY"!

LOTS OF GOOD STUFF IN HERE! LIKE **THIS**: "MAY 25TH — THAT MARK KESSLER IS SO **CUTE**! HOPE HE'S MY PARTNER ON THE SCIENCE PROJECT!"

AH! ISN'T THE HONESTY **TOUCHING**? JUST A GIRL, A PEN AND HER DEEPEST, MOST PRIVATE THOUGHTS!

YES, THERE'S NOTHING LIKE A DIARY FOR CHRONICLING ALL THE SIGNIFICANT EVENTS OF—

... CHILDHOOD.

P O W

August 8th— Turning in early. Bad headache.

"A RAKE'S PROGRESS"

Sigh...

HI, MR. EUSTIS! IT'S THAT TIME OF YEAR AGAIN!

WHAT TIME OF YEAR?

LEAF-RAKING TIME! WANT ME TO DO YOUR LAWN?

NATE, I HIRED YOU TO DO MY LAWN **LAST** YEAR.

...AND AS I RECALL, YOU DIDN'T GET AROUND TO IT UNTIL THERE WAS **SNOW** ON THE GROUND!

THAT WAS AN ORGANIZATIONAL PROBLEM! THAT WON'T HAPPEN **THIS** YEAR!

I'VE GOT A **SYSTEM** NOW! I WRITE EVERYTHING DOWN ON THESE SLIPS OF PAPER!

SEE? NAMES! DATES! I'VE GOT IT ALL RIGHT HERE! THAT WAY, **THIS** YEAR WON'T BE LIKE **LAST** YEAR!

ALL THE YEARS ARE STARTING TO SEEM ALIKE.

by Lincoln Peirce

✳ SIGH... ✳

FOUND IT!

WANT ME TO LOOK FOR YOUR BALL, TOO?

NO

by
Lincoln
Peirce

Time once again for the adventures of...
SUPERDAD!
...the world's **ONLY** bald superhero! (with a slight paunch)

And introducing dim-witted sidekick...
MegaTEEN!
Dang
She fights crime... **AND** chronic acne!

One fine day...
Ye **GADS!**
What **IS** it, Superdad?

It's that fiend **GARBAGE-MAN!** He's coming up the street!
ALREADY? It's not even 8:00 AM!

The devious devil! He **knows** we're not ready for him!
What will we **DO?**

What else?...
dramatic pause
TAKE OUT THE GARBAGE!
Um... what are you looking at **ME** for?

Well, **I** certainly can't do it! Not with my bulging disk!
Well, I can't either! Garbage is so smelly and **GROSS!**

Then that means this is a job for...
CHORE-BOY!

NATE!